GHOST STORIES
of the FIRST WORLD WAR

Maria Da Silva & Andrew Hind

GHOST
HOUSE

Ghost House Books

© 2014 by Ghost House Books
First printed in 2014 10 9 8 7 6 5 4 3 2 1
Printed in China

The Distributor: Lone Pine Publishing
87 East Pender Street
Vancouver, BC V6A 1S9
Canada

Websites: www.ghostbooks.net
           www.lonepinepublishing.com

Library and Archives Canada Cataloguing in Publication

Da Silva, Maria, author
         Ghost stories of the First World War / Maria Da Silva and Andrew
Hind.

Includes bibliographical references.

ISBN 978-1-55105-911-2 (pbk.)

         1. World War, 1914-1918. 2. Legends. I. Hind, Andrew, author
II. Title.

D523.D23 2014   940.3   C2014-903085-1

Editorial Director: Nancy Foulds
Project Editor: Sheila Cooke
Production Manager: Leslie Hung
Layout and Production: Volker Bodegom, Alesha Braitenbach
Cover Design: Gerry Dotto
Front and Back Cover Images: © Photos.com / Thinkstock
Image Credits: authors' collection: 85, 213, 214; Library and Archives Canada
15; Niagara Historical Museum 52; The Wartime Memories Project 37;
Wikimedia Commons 13, 27, 110, 122, 143, 149, 166, 168, 178.

We acknowledge the financial support of the Government of Canada through
the Canada Book Fund (CBF) for our publishing activities.

Canadian   Patrimoine
Heritage   canadien

PC: 27

Dedication

This book is dedicated to the memory of Harry Hind,
255th Overseas Battalion (Q.O.R.), C.E.F.

Preface

Although many people associate ghost stories with tall tales and wildly imaginative yarns meant to frighten and chill, this book is not a work of fiction. It details true hauntings from across the globe, all of which are tied to the First World War (sometimes called the Great War). By true, we mean that every story collected within this volume has a strong tradition or historical foundation upon which to rest, and came from eyewitnesses who swore the experiences they recounted were factual—these stories are certainly true to those who reported them. We cannot prove beyond the shadow of a doubt that any of these tales involves entities that somehow defy the supposedly one-way road souls take after death, but we think it's possible they do.

We also attempted to recount the experiences as told to us with little artistic licence. It's our belief that while ghost stories should be dramatic, they should also be truthfully presented and, as much as possible, authenticated. We extensively researched every story in this book using archival material, newspapers and interviews with knowledgeable individuals. The most strenuous efforts have been made for accuracy, both in historical detail and in the retelling of our sources' paranormal encounters.

This book has been laid to rest (so to speak), but our explorations of the strange and the mysterious certainly have not come to an end. If you know a haunting or unusual tale, or have experienced something paranormal yourself, please contact us by looking us up online.

In the meantime, enjoy the book. Just be sure to keep the lights on.

Contents

Introduction

Dawn breaks over the ghostly landscape of skeletal trees and shattered remains of farmhouses jutting from the ground like tombstones. The whole sky lights up suddenly as an artillery bombardment pounds the enemy lines. Grim soldiers, covered in mud, nervously wait in trenches for the order to attack. A whistle blows and, as one, the men rise up, throw themselves out of the trench and begin to race across the barren land toward the distant enemy.

Bullets whip by like swarms of angry hornets, and soldiers begin to fall. Even among the din of battle—the roar of exploding artillery shells, the crackle of machine guns, officers shouting orders—the pitiful cries of the wounded and dying can be distinctly heard. The attackers dwindle in number with each metre advanced, and still they press onward into the storm of bullets and artillery. A tangle of barbed wire fencing appears in the gloom ahead. Like flies on a spider's web, dozens of corpses are suspended within it, victims of a previous attack. Their uniforms are in tatters, their helmets sit atop skulls stripped of their flesh, and their skeletal hands claw up at the sky.

Halted by this grim obstacle, the soldiers dive into shell holes to escape the carnage. There, they are greeted by more ashen-faced corpses staring blankly ahead. As shells continue to explode around them, the cowering soldiers press their hands to their ears to drown out the chaos. Then they recoil in horror as the corpses begin to stir: the dead confront the living, turning their lifeless gazes accusingly on the soldiers…

Welcome to the battlefields of World War I, where the living and dead mingled together, where terror was a constant companion, and where ghosts of the fallen rose in such numbers as to create spectral armies. Was the wraith-like figure sharing your shell crater a soldier near death, or was he the apparition of someone who had already passed over that barrier? One often could not tell.

For most people, death is a release, a passage into the just rewards of the afterlife. Yet not everyone who dies rests easy. Some, usually those whose end came prematurely, who left unfinished business or who died in some tragic manner, stubbornly refuse to cross over to the other side. It should come as little surprise that World War I saw an explosion of ghostly experiences. In that horrific conflict, millions of young men died never having experienced all that life promises, their bodies torn apart by artillery, shot through with bullets or ravaged by poison gas or disease.

If even a fraction of these men rose from their graves as lost souls, we're talking a veritable army of spectres and wraiths haunting the battlefields, cemeteries and other locations stained by the blood of war. And when it came to researching this volume, that's exactly what we found: countless tales involving bizarre apparitions, unexplained phenomena and life-saving premonitions emerged from a century of hiding like a wave of soldiers going "over the top" of their trenches.

Cultural acceptance of the supernatural predates World War I. In the 50 years before the conflict, there had been a turn toward spiritualism with the Spiritualist movement in Europe and North America. The attempt to understand the great beyond, to communicate with those who had passed on, and to make sense of one's own mortality drove people to embrace spiritualism and the supernatural. Most of these people were educated and came from the middle and upper classes; this movement wasn't a case of the naïve, unlearned or superstitious being taken in by spiritual mediums, but rather owing to a widespread belief that the occult was an enlightenment of sorts. Spiritualists actually saw themselves as forward thinking and their movement as expanding human horizons.

Séances were the means of communication with the dead, with mediums often acting as a channel through which the living "spoke" with spirits of the deceased. Although it was widely accepted, communication with the dead was intensely personal and was generally conducted in one's home and among close friends. There were also numerous secret societies that embraced occultism and would have included spirit communication among their mysterious rites and rituals.

World War I marked an important turning point in the Spiritualist movement. Death was ever-present in the early 20th century—disease, workplace accidents, childhood mortality and illnesses only poorly understood by medicine meant families then were more frequently touched by death than our own today—but the mass deaths as a result of trench warfare left millions of families grieving and seeking closure. Bereavement often preceded spiritual exploration.

The interest in and acceptance of spiritualism as a means of understanding death and what lies beyond was mirrored by soldiers on the battlefields. The grim and brutal nature of a soldier's existence in the Great War saw belief in the paranormal explode. The dead mingled with the living on the battlefields, so that the barrier between life and death blurred. The strange was made ordinary, death was natural and life was fleeting.

Soldiers accepted the supernatural as a means of making sense of their wartime experiences. Whereas for many of us witnessing a formless spirit would be terrifying, enough to force us to disbelieve the event merely to retain our sanity, for the soldiers of World War I, a ghostly encounter might pale in comparison to the horrors of the battlefield. It was often nearly impossible to tell a grimy, exhausted, mud-caked, sleeping soldier from a corpse. The familiarity with death, the unrelenting carnage and the realization that a man could be felled in the blink of an eye encouraged a heightened awareness of the thin line between this life and the next.

During those nearly five years of horror and death, countless men claimed to have seen dead comrades resurrected and wandering the scarred battlefields, or vengeful spirits emerging from shell holes driven by an insatiable hunger for the souls of the living. In other cases, soldiers claimed to have seen angels hovering over the battlefield, felt an otherworldly presence that somehow silenced enemy guns just for a little while, or had portents of doom come in time to save lives.

And the paranormal wasn't limited to battlefields. Those left behind on the homefront had their share of unexplainable experiences as well. UFOs flying over Canadian cities, spectral ships arriving in port weeks after they had been sent to the bottom of the Atlantic, and fallen soldiers who returned from overseas to say a final goodbye.

Ghost Stories of the First World War is our attempt to chronicle some of the more spine-tingling, heart-wrenching and gripping of the countless "grave" tales to come out of World War I.

Overview of the First World War

Ghost Stories of the First World War is, as the title suggests, a collection of some of the supernatural tales associated with World War I (1914–1918). By their very nature, most of the haunting stories herein involve, to some degree or another, battles and military campaigns. Without knowing the wider context of events in which these tales take place, it's difficult to fully appreciate or comprehend them. But sometimes, details can distract from the true narrative—the tragedy of individuals whose souls cannot find peace after death. It would be particularly easy to feel hopelessly lost and out of one's depth in the case of a war that literally spanned the globe, with dozens of battles in diverse campaigns ranging from the cold waters of the North Atlantic and the dizzying heights of the Alps to the steaming jungles of Africa and the trackless sands of the Middle East. We knew we didn't want to bog readers down with too much extraneous historical detail within the stories themselves, but we also recognize that there is nothing more frustrating than having to put down a book to track down an unfamiliar reference.

Our solution was to include a chapter that details, in brief, the path the Great War took over four-and-a-half long years of fighting. Anyone who wishes to look elsewhere for greater detail on the battles, campaigns and personalities of the war is encouraged to do so, but for the casual reader, this chapter should suffice for an overview of the course of the conflict. Of course, while we believe a general understanding of the war enhances one's appreciation of the ghosts stories it bred, those who have little interest in military history can feel free to skip this chapter.

A Brief Summary

Although the June 28, 1914, assassination of the heir to the Austro-Hungarian throne by a Serbian national was the event that sparked the Great War, international tensions had been building for many years. When Austria-Hungary declared war on Serbia on July 28, Russia began to mobilize troops against Austria-Hungary and her German ally. As per long-standing treaty stipulations, France and Britain joined the war in support of Russia.

Soon, much of the world was embroiled in the conflict. On the one side were the so-called Central Powers, including Austria-Hungary, Germany, the Ottoman Empire (Turkey) and Bulgaria. Opposing them were the Allies: Russia, Britain and France (and their globe-spanning empires), Canada, Australia, Belgium, Serbia, Montenegro, Italy, Romania, Portugal and Japan. In 1917, the war turned irrecoverably against the Central Powers when the United States entered on the Allied side.

The Treaty of Versailles, signed in 1919, changed the geographic face of Europe, and indeed much of the world (the Ottoman Empire was broken up to create new Middle East nations, and German overseas colonies in Africa and the Pacific were assumed by Britain, France and Japan), and brought about numerous political, economic and social changes. Warfare had seen the introduction of tanks, airplanes and poison gas. Russia had become a Communist state. But most dramatically, the war had seen the deaths of more than 10 million persons and the grievous injuring of millions more.

The assassination of Austrian Archduke Franz Ferdinand was the spark that ignited World War I.

The Western Front

When one thinks of World War I, it's generally the muddy fields and corpse-strewn trenches of northern France and Belgium that come to mind. The Western Front was the decisive theatre of the war, and the most horrific.

The conflict began in early August with a rapid German advance through Belgium and northeastern France that was only stopped by the French and British at the First Battle of the Marne in September 1914. By December, both sides had dug into a series of fortified trenches stretching from the English Channel to the Swiss border. This battle line remained almost stationary for the next four years as generals struggled to find ways to create a breakthrough and succeeded only in throwing their armies into a series of costly but futile battles. Waves of soldiers were sent out of the trenches ("over the top"), only to be caught up in barbed wire or shot down by machine guns. Successes were measured in metres.

The battles that defined the war were fought on the Western Front. The names Somme, Ypres, Verdun, Passchendaele, Vimy Ridge and Argonne resonate to this day, echoing human tragedy on an unimaginable scale. A generation of German, French and British and Imperial troops was literally bled white in those muddy, shell-cratered fields.

Finally, after three-and-a-half years of stalemate, a German offensive in July 1918 almost achieved the long sought-after decisive breakthrough, but the Allies held, if just barely. This attack, designed to win the war before the full weight of the newly involved United States could be brought to bear, finally depleted the strength of the worn-out German army. An Allied counterattack later in the year pushed the German soldiers back almost to their borders, broke the will of the German populace to resist and brought the war to a close on November 11, 1918.

Millions of young men heeded the call and enlisted, only to be caught up in the horrors of trench warfare.

The Eastern Front

When Austria-Hungary declared war on Serbia on July 28, 1914, Russia began to mobilize its armies in support of Serbia. Three days later, Germany sided with Austria-Hungary against Russia. To kick off the war in the east, Russian troops invaded East Prussia (part of the German empire) but were soundly defeated at both the Battle of Tannenberg (August 29–30, 1914) and the Battle of Masurian Lakes (September 9–14, 1914). Russia had more success against Austria-Hungary by invading Galicia (southeastern Poland and western Ukraine) and capturing the city of Lemberg (Lvov).

In May 1915, it was the German and Austro-Hungarian armies' turn to strike back, routing the Russians in Galicia and retaking Lemberg. The Germans followed up by driving the Russians from Poland and Lithuania. Russian offensives against Austria-Hungary in 1916 met with some success but were not decisive enough to rescue her flagging fortunes.

Time ran out on the corrupt and inept Russian monarchy. With the army facing defeat after defeat on the battlefield, and her civilian population on the verge of starvation, the nation was ripe for an upheaval. In March 1917, the tsar's regime was toppled, and the new Russian government quickly made peace and withdrew from the war. It wasn't long before the Communists took over, murdering the royal family and transforming Russia into the Soviet Union. The seeds of the Cold War were planted on the battlefields of World War I.

The War in Africa

By 1914, the European powers' 19th-century "scramble for Africa" had created a patchwork of colonies blanketing the entire African continent. Britain, France, Belgium, Italy, Portugal and Germany each had extensive colonies.

The war in Europe quickly spread to these African colonies. With Britain, France, Belgium, Italy and Portugal allied against Germany, the scattered German colonies in what are today Tanzania, Cameroon, Togo and Namibia were vulnerable targets for invasion. Although the military forces in Africa were significantly smaller and less well-armed than the massive, powerful armies on the Western Front, the fighting, which featured European as well as native African troops, was no less deadly.

In August 1914, Allied forces invaded German Togoland, German Cameroon and German Southwest Africa. Each one quickly fell. British commanders turned their attention to the largest and most important colony, German East Africa, in November 1914. There, the vastly outnumbered and undersupplied German army, headed by General Lettow-Vorbeck, pursued a brilliant campaign to the continued embarrassment of the Allies. With only 3000 troops, the general tied up as many as 100,000 Allied troops at a time for more than four years and was never defeated, only surrendering when the Armistice had been signed in Europe, bringing the war to a close.

Notably, the greatest cause of death in Africa was not enemy action but rather illness and disease. For example, during the campaign in East Africa, of 62,000 British casualties, almost 49,000 were caused by disease.

The War in Egypt and Palestine

Egypt was a protectorate of Britain, and her Suez Canal was a vital lifeline to Britain's Asian colonies and had to be protected at all costs. As soon as the Ottoman Empire announced it was entering the war against the Allies, it began making preparations to invade Egypt. The first attempt was made in February 1915, but the Turks were repelled with heavy losses. To protect the Suez, Britain began an advance through Egypt that steadily pushed back Ottoman forces. By December 1916, they were on the borders of Palestine, and the Suez Canal was no longer in danger.

The British could have stopped there, but instead they continued to pursue their enemy into Palestine. Jerusalem was too tempting a prize to ignore. After much hard fighting over difficult terrain and in bad weather, the Holy City fell on December 8, 1917. The Turks were pushed back into Syria, and Palestine became a British protectorate after centuries of Turkish rule.

The War in Mesopotamia

Shortly after the Ottoman Empire allied itself with Germany and entered the war in November 1914, Britain sent a force from India to Mesopotamia (Iraq) to secure its oil interests in neighbouring Iran. The troops were then ordered to move northward to capture Baghdad. At first the British were successful, but they were eventually driven into Kut-el-Amara, where they were surrounded and besieged. After a 143-day attack, the British surrendered in April 1916.

British reinforcements were rushed to the Persian Gulf, and a renewed effort was made to take Baghdad. The Turks were destroyed at the climactic Battle of Kut and were chased north, through Baghdad and beyond. By war's end, all of Mesopotamia was in British hands.

The Mesopotamian campaign was not of great strategic value, but it did deal the Ottoman Empire a blow from which it never recovered, and the fall of the mystical city of Baghdad boosted Allied morale at a time when it was sagging.

The Italian Front

Italy remained neutral until May 23, 1915, when it decided to join the Allies and fight its traditional enemy, Austria-Hungary. The fighting was limited to the rugged mountains of northeastern Italy, a difficult region in which to wage war. The Italian army took the offensive in the Isonzo River valley, but the Austrians had already fortified the mountains there, and the Italians were unable to make any headway. In 1916, it was Austria's turn to launch an offensive, this one aimed at Venice. It very nearly succeeded. The offensive so weakened Austria, however, that Italian assaults later that year and in 1917 threatened to knock the Austro-Hungarian Empire from the war.

Fearing the loss of her ally, Germany rushed reinforcements to the Italian Front and turned the tide. At the Battle of Caporetto, the Italian army was defeated, and the ensuing retreat rapidly became a rout. Only with Allied assistance was the Central Powers' offensive finally halted.

In November 1918, after being defeated at the Battle of Vittoria Veneto, the Austrians sued for peace, and under the peace terms handed Trieste over to Italy.

The War in the Balkans

Although World War I began when the Austro-Hungarian Empire declared war on Serbia, the Balkans were something of a sideshow in the ensuing conflict. Bulgaria joined the Central Powers and teamed up with Austria to dismember Serbia, Montenegro and Albania.

Romania wavered for two years, unsure of which side (if either) to take before finally taking the side of the Allies and declaring war on the Central Powers in August 1916. After brief initial success in invading Hungarian Transylvania (a traditional part of Romania), Romania found herself overrun by Bulgarian and German armies.

Greece was inevitably pulled into the war as well. A French and British expeditionary force in Salonica, in northern Greece, ensured that Greece retained its neutrality. At the same time, the Allies seized the Greek navy, large stores of ammunition from the army and the railways and telegraph system, and blockaded her coast.

In September 1918, the Salonica force moved against Bulgaria in Macedonia. Within two weeks, Bulgaria was suing for peace. The Allies then liberated both Serbia and Montenegro.

The Assassination of Archduke Franz Ferdinand

The young Serb fingered the pistol concealed in his jacket pocket. There was a round in the chamber and the magazine was full. He was in the Bosnian capital of Sarajevo to kill Austrian Archduke Franz Ferdinand. He watched with barely concealed malice as the Archduke and his wife waved at the crowds as they were driven through the streets of the city Austria-Hungary had recently annexed. The assassin felt a new wave of hatred for the archduke and for Austria boil up inside him. He knew there would be terrible repercussions for what he was about to do, but he took comfort in the fact that he would send a powerful message to Austria.

The people lining the street cheered and applauded as the car passed slowly through the narrow streets. The combined voices created a racket that shook the Serb like an artillery barrage. How could these people cheer for this man? Was he not the symbol of an oppressor?

Filled with hatred, the man acted. He pulled the gun from his pocket and jumped from the crowd into the street. The car was right there. Leaping onto the running board, he aimed the gun and pulled the trigger. A bullet screamed into the archduke's neck. He seized up, his handsome face distorted by pain. The archduke slumped to the seat in a pool of blood just as a second bullet struck his beloved wife in the stomach, fatally wounding her.

The crowd exploded in a wild panic. The assassin, stunned that he had succeeded in his mission, watched numbly as uniformed policemen raced toward him and didn't fight or offer any resistance as he was tackled to the ground. In his mind, he had struck a blow against the hated Austro-Hungarian Empire, sending a message that Bosnia belonged to the Serbs.

What he couldn't know was that the June 28, 1914, assassination would strike a match to the powder keg upon which Europe sat, causing an explosion in the form of a war that would kill 10 million people. And even if he had foreseen the possibility that it would spark such a conflict, how could the young assassin have possibly imagined that these murders would also give birth to a chilling paranormal legacy that would haunt Europe well after the guns of World War I had fallen silent and the soldiers returned home from their muddy trenches?

In a nightmarish twist to one of history's most infamous events, the luxury automobile in which Archduke Franz Ferdinand and his wife were slain became subject to a ghastly curse that saw the vehicle injure, maim or kill out-right a long string of owners in the decades afterward, leaving in its path a trail of bloodshed and horror. The accursed automobile, its exquisite beauty belying the evil spirit trapped within its metal frame, is today a centrepiece attraction in the Vienna Military Museum (Heeresgeschichtliches Museum), where it can no longer do any harm. But is the car truly at rest, or is its hunger for mayhem merely temporarily sated?

It isn't just the limo that was scarred by that tragic event of June 1914. According to the persistent legend, the stretch of road along which the Austro-Hungarian royals were gunned down is horribly tainted as well. In the years since, locals have reported bizarre phenomena along the street: sightings of ethereal ghosts and phantom vehicles; the spine-chilling sounds of pained screams and cries of terror splitting the night's silence; and tension that creeps into the air for no apparent reason. It's as if somehow the restless spirits of the Austrian royals coalesce at the very spot where they were slain to infuse the atmosphere with their suffering.

It all began with 20-year-old Gavrilo Princip, who desperately wanted Archduke Franz Ferdinand dead. A Bosnian-Serbian nationalist and member of the terrorist organization Young Bosnia, Princip hated the Austro-Hungarian Empire for having annexed his native province of Bosnia-Herzegovina in 1908. When Princip learned that the heir to the despised throne was to visit the Bosnian capital of Sarajevo, he and his companions began plotting Franz Ferdinand's assassination. But Princip and his friends were students, not trained revolutionaries, and it wasn't long before their plans were uncovered by Colonel Dragutin Dimitrijevic, a member of Serbian military intelligence. Rather than break up the plot, however, Dimitrijevic, who was also secretly the leader of the Black Hand, a Serbian terrorist organization tasked with reclaiming the historical Serbian territories currently held by Austria-Hungary, saw an opportunity.

The Austro-Hungarian occupation of Bosnia angered Serbia, which considered the tiny province a Serbian homeland. Dimitrijevic decided to sponsor Princip and his fellow plotters. The youthful Bosnian nationalists offered a way for Serbia to strike at their ancient enemy while keeping their own hands clean. Dimitrijevic therefore supplied Princip and his companions with pistols and bombs, as well as cyanide pills to be used in the event of capture to ensure they couldn't be forced to implicate anyone. The young assassins were then transported from Belgrade to Sarajevo, where they awaited the arrival of the archduke.

Many in the Austrian court tried to convince Franz Ferdinand not to visit Sarajevo. A series of eerie premonitions suggested that to go to Bosnia would be a grave mistake. Years before, a gypsy fortune teller had seen in her cards a terrible future wherein the archduke "would one day let loose a world war." Then, during a hunting trip in 1913, Franz Ferdinand accidentally shot a rare white stag. He and his hunting party gasped in horror when the deer fell—it was widely believed that anyone who killed such an animal would die or lose a loved one within a year. The incident seemed to haunt the archduke, and he began to have his own premonitions of an early end. He apparently told confidants mere months before his death, "I know I shall soon be murdered," and the doomed man became extremely depressed and full of foreboding as 1914 progressed.

Franz Ferdinand was no coward, however, and he put official duty above personal safety. So the state visit to Sarajavo would go forward as planned. A Graf & Stift Double Phaeton automobile was selected to transport the royals through the city. The Austrian-built phaeton was a large, sleek, six-passenger convertible limousine with a powerful four-cylinder engine custom built for exclusive clientele.

Although some in the archduke's entourage were concerned that the open-topped vehicle left Franz Ferdinand and his wife dangerously exposed in a province seething with emotions, others felt it offered an opportunity for the royals to connect with the crowds in a way an enclosed vehicle wouldn't. Certainly the elegant automobile befitted royalty—in fact, many members of the Austrian Imperial Court owned that model—and would surely impress the population. Any concerns regarding the vulnerability of the vehicle were put aside in the name of creating a grand spectacle.

On June 28, 1914, Franz Ferdinand and his wife, Countess Sophie, arrived in Sarajevo. Initially, it looked as though their concerns were unfounded. As the six-car motorcade drove through streets lined with spectators and at least 120 vigilant police officers, most of the awaiting assassins quickly lost their nerve and fled. There was no sign of trouble as the imperial motorcade wound its way toward the city's centre; the crowd was calm and peaceful.

Suddenly, at 10:10 AM, one of Princip's fellow conspirators, 19-year-old Nedeljko Cabrinovic, stepped from the masses, armed his bomb and threw it at the archduke's vehicle. The device bounced off the hood, sailed over the heads of Franz Ferdinand and his wife and exploded beneath the following car. The explosion ripped through the vehicle, left a crater in the road and injured several members of the imperial entourage as well as some innocent bystanders. As police converged on the shattered remains of the vehicle to tend to the wounded, the car carrying the archduke sped ahead to get the royals out of danger. Now travelling at high speed, the motorcade screamed past the three other assassins lining the route, none of whom had time to act.

Arriving safely at the scheduled stop at City Hall, where he was to address local dignitaries, Franz Ferdinand was furious that there had been an attempt on his life. Anger drowned out his good sense. The practical thing to do would be to retire as quickly as possible to a secure location, but Franz Ferdinand instead cut short his speech and insisted on being driven to the hospital to visit those who had been wounded in the bombing. Some of his entourage begged him to reconsider. The narrow, winding streets of the old city presented too many opportunities for other assassins to make an attempt on his life. It was too risky, they argued. But the archduke would hear nothing of it.

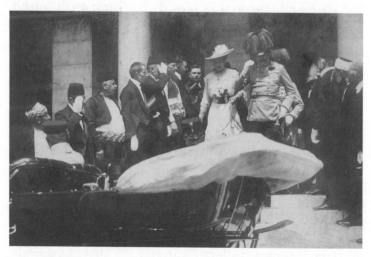

Archduke Franz Ferdinand and his wife, Countess Sophie, in Sarajevo on the day of their assassination.

As it happened, Franz Ferdinand's driver got lost on his way to the hospital. Realizing he had made a wrong turn, the chaffeur was backing off of Latin Bridge and just heading onto Rudolph Street when Princip happened upon the scene. By now, Princip had learned that the bombing had failed to kill its intended target. All of a sudden, the archduke was right before him, a virtually stationary target. It was a remarkable example of good fortune for him, and sheer bad luck for the royals.

Swallowing his fear, Princip raced up to the car and jumped onto its running board. There, from point-blank range, he shot the startled Franz Ferdinand through the neck, severing his jugular vein. Countess Sophie barely had time to cry out in horror before the young fanatic fired again, his second shot striking her in the abdomen. There was blood everywhere. The archduke reached for his wife and, through a mouth frothing with blood, begged her not to slip away. "Sophie, Sophie, don't die. Stay alive for the children!" Moments later, he lost consciousness. The archduke and his wife were rushed away to get medical attention, but both died within minutes. There was nothing any doctor could have done to save either of them.

The assassination of Archduke Franz Ferdinand and Countess Sophie had far-reaching consequences. Austria-Hungary understandably held Serbia responsible, but made unreasonable demands on Serbia as punishment and compensation. When Serbia refused to comply, Austria-Hungary declared war and invaded. A complex network of alliances quickly drew in most of Europe. As countries mobilized against one another, the globe slid inexorably into the most brutal, bloody and costly war the world had ever seen. Approximately 10 million people would perish before the guns finally fell silent in 1918. Very few events in the 20th century had the shattering impact of the assassination of Archduke Franz Ferdinand.

Some of the horror of the moments immediately following the shooting—when the dying royals clung to one another, rage-fuelled individuals tackled the assassin and panicked onlookers ran from the sound of gunfire—seemed to cling to the archduke's car. Just as Franz Ferdinand and Sophie's blood stained its seats and floor, so too did the emotional weight of the double murder and the war it sparked stain the luxury automobile. It became a cursed vehicle, beautiful yet deadly, a wolf in sheep's clothing. All owners thereafter either had their lives cut short or were injured in mysterious accidents. In the next dozen years, the automobile was owned by 15 people, was involved in six accidents and took the lives of at least 13 individuals.

The car's first victim following the assasination was its owner, General Potiorek, the Governor of Bosnia-Herzegovina. He was with the archduke and his wife on the day they were shot. He had watched helplessly as they died. When war was declared against Serbia, Potiorek was placed in command of the invading army. Unfortunately, he performed poorly at the battles of Cer and Kolubara, helping ensure that the war started badly for the Austro-Hungarian Empire. Emperor Franz Josef called for the general to return to Vienna to answer for his failures. Stripped of command, his reputation in tatters, humiliated before his peers and wracked by the guilt of failing to protect the royals in the province he governed, Potiorek went into a dark depression. His health took a precipitous decline and he became suicidal. He never recovered.

When Potiorek was recalled to Vienna in 1915, he sold his automobile to a captain on his staff. Less than 10 days after taking possession, the officer was involved in a horrific accident. While racing along a winding country road, he struck and killed two peasants and then crashed into a tree. The impact threw the captain from the vehicle, his body landing broken and lifeless more than 10 metres away.

The next owner encountered a string of four unfortunate accidents in the span of only four months, the last of them leaving one of his arms crippled. Convinced the car was cursed, he felt the vehicle should be destroyed. His friend, a doctor named Srikis, disagreed.

Scoffing at the notion that a car could carry a dark curse, Dr. Srikis saw only a beautiful automobile that would make him the envy of his friends and peers. He purchased it and drove it proudly for six months, oblivious to the fact that death, not the hands of man, shifted the automobile's gears. Then one day the overturned vehicle was found in a roadside ditch, Dr. Srikis crushed beneath it. The car had claimed yet another life.

Another doctor became the next owner, but by now the car had developed a dire reputation. When the superstitious patients of the doctor learned of the transaction, they began to desert him in droves. They wanted nothing to do with a man connected to an object of darkness. With his clientele deserting him, the doctor had no choice but to sell the phaeton.

Taking possession was a Swiss racecar driver. He didn't get to enjoy the car's majesty for long; he met a grisly death when, in a race through the Dolomite Mountains, he lost control, was thrown from the car and broke his neck. The next owner, a diamond dealer, died untimely as well…by his own hands when he pressed a gun to his temple and pulled the trigger.

A wealthy Serbian landowner who morbidly admired the car's historical significance paid a hefty amount of money to own it next. He paid no heed to warnings about a curse. All he could think of was how proud he would be to drive the car in which the heirs of the hated Austro-Hungarian Empire were murdered. Not long afterward, he perished when he crashed into a horse cart.

The final owner was a Serbian garage owner. While returning from a wedding, he found himself behind a long line of slow-moving cars. Impatient, perhaps fuelled by too much celebratory wine, he slammed his foot down on the gas pedal and swerved into the oncoming lane to pass. About half of the cars were behind him when his eyes suddenly went wide at the sight of an approaching vehicle rounding a corner ahead. Unable to squeeze back into his lane, the driver had no choice but to swerve off the road to avoid a collision. Unfortunately, he lost control and the car slammed into a tree at high speed. The driver (and some sources say several other celebrants in the vehicle) died in the mangled wreck.

Following that final accident, the car was committed to a museum in Austria, where it was put on exhibit to be gawked at by throngs of visitors filled with morbid curiosity. The roads of southeastern Europe have been safer ever since.

Sharp-eyed museum-goers may notice an astounding coincidence concerning the "death limo," as it has since become known. The Armistice that signalled the end of the First World War occurred on November 11, 1918. Incredibly, the vehicle's licence plate reads "AIII 118," or A (for Armistice) 11–11–18. Not only did the car provide the spark that would burst into the flames of a global war, but its licence plate seems to have predicted the war's end as well. While this may simply be one of the most eerie, jaw-dropping coincidences of all time, perhaps there is something more to it…

Meanwhile, the Sarajevo street where Archduke Franz Ferdinand and Countess Sophie were murdered has been a place of macabre interest for decades, and many tourists have driven or walked by the infamous location. The barrier between past and present, dead and living, is as flimsy as a cheap wooden door here, and sometimes that door swings wide open. People often speak of a foreboding feeling that results in lingering unease, as if something you can't quite put your finger on is terribly wrong. Others have reported witnessing the silent apparitions of the doomed couple reliving the final moments of their lives or staring out into nothingness with dead eyes as a phantom car from another era races past. The silence of the hours after midnight is sometimes broken by the sounds of gunfire, a woman's sobbing and screams of anguish, with no discernible source.

Late one night, sometime in the 1990s, a Sarajevo man was driving down the street when he saw a pair of lights speeding toward him. The oncoming lights suddenly veered into his path. The man yelled out in surprise, honked the horn and slammed on the brakes. The oncoming vehicle straightened out just moments before a collision. In the glare of the headlights, the startled driver noticed the other car was a beautiful antique convertible. As the car passed by, the man was horrified to see no driver behind its wheel, but two shadowy figures seated in the back. As soon as the vehicle passed, it disappeared—watching through his rearview mirror, the driver claimed it simply vanished. It didn't turn a corner or fade into the distance; it was just swallowed by the darkness.

This man's horror isn't unique. Over the years, others have had unexplainable encounters with a spectral vehicle along that very street. In one terrifying episode, an eye-witness watched as a pair of human-shaped shadows detached themselves from the car as it passed. These shadows had no source, nothing from which they could have been cast. They flickered and danced like sputtering candles, long arms stretching out along the walls as if reaching for something beyond their grasp. Shivers shuddered through the eyewitness as a supernatural chill descended.

Are these shadows the lost souls of Archduke Franz Ferdinand and his wife, Countess Sophie, attempting to complete a journey left unfinished in June 1914? Is the spec-tral car seen speeding down the Sarajevo street the spectral remnant of their limo attempting to outrun death?

Few events have impacted history as heavily or resulted in a more chilling paranormal legacy. The car in which the heirs to the Austro-Hungarian throne were murdered took on a menacing life of its own, becoming hungry for more death and mayhem, feeding on the souls of those it had maimed and murdered. The street in Sarajevo where the tragedy occurred has been similarly altered by the misery and pain of that fateful summer day a century ago—and of the ghastly war it ignited.

If you visit either, keep your wits about you. Terror is never far away.

Phantom Pilot of Netheravon

The airfield at Netheravon, located 25 kilometres north of Salisbury in Wiltshire, England, has been home to a number of milestones in British military aviation. Over the course of the past century it has had a hand in the birth of each of the Royal Air Force (RAF), the Royal Navy's Fleet Air Arm and the Army Air Corps. Yet its legacy is not all of glory and achievement. A dark stain taints the base, one that simply refuses to fade despite the passage of time. This lingering mark, unseen by most but which infuses the airfield with a melancholy air, manifests as a tragic spirit who walks the grounds and lurks within the shadows of the aged buildings, searching in vain for a life that was prematurely snuffed out.

The air base at Netheravon was founded in 1912, before the RAF or even its predecessor, the Royal Flying Corps (RFC), was established. That year, the Air Battalion, Royal Engineers, took over some Army Cavalry School buildings located just outside of the sleepy village of Netheravon. The engineers laid out two grass runways, designated as North and South Airfields. A year later, the newly formed RFC took possession, and on June 16, 1913, No. 3 Squadron moved in. Soon, the airfields were filled with aircraft, and residents of the nearby village grew accustomed to the constant droning of planes flying overhead. A small community of messes, hangars, barracks and other buildings began to take shape on the base. Some of these timeworn buildings remain in use today, a century later.

With the onset of the Great War, the airfield expanded greatly to meet the demands of the rapidly expanding RFC. Together with the Central Flying School at Upavon, Netheravon was one of Britain's main training bases for new pilots learning to operate their aircraft. In order to prepare pilots for the rigours and realities of aerial combat over the Western Front, training was thorough and intense. Unfortunately, rigorous and realistic training occasionally resulted in accidents—through pilot error or mechanical failure—and many youthful pilots died before ever seeing combat.

At the end of the First World War, the RFC became the Royal Air Force, and Netheravon became home to No. 1 Flying Training School. The routine of training pilots for service continued uninterrupted. For the first decade of its existence, the airfield was, well, normal. But a chilly night in the 1920s changed the mood to something distinctly paranormal.

It was four or five years after the war had ended when a young pilot-in-training, whose name is being withheld upon request of his granddaughter relating the story to us today, awoke with a start in the middle of the night. He instinctively knew something was wrong. It took a moment for his eyes to clear and adjust to the darkness in the barracks, but when they did he gasped in shock. Looming over him was a shadowy figure wearing slightly outdated pilot's gear. The collar of his thigh-length leather coat was pulled up high to the ears, a scarf was wound around his neck and a leather helmet and goggles topped his head. The startled trainee's eyes settled upon the embroidered crest sewn onto the eerily silent figure's breast: the letters "RFC" between a pair of white wings. No one had worn that crest since the Royal Flying Corps became the Royal Air Force in 1918.

The pilot trainee glanced around the room. The other young airmen who should have been asleep in their bunks were nowhere to be seen. The beds were empty, the blankets pulled tight as if they had not been slept in at all that night. To his horror, the young pilot realized the barracks were strangely empty except for himself and the shadowy figure standing over him. *My friends! Where are my friends?* Panic started to well up inside him. *What the bloody hell is going on? Where is everyone?*

Almost paralyzed with fear, he struggled to turn his head and return his eyes to the dark figure looming over his bed, intently staring down at him. The young man couldn't see the apparition's face clearly: its features were hidden behind a smoky haze that seemed to glow with a faint white light. The figure simply stood there, unmoving, intimidating in silence.

The 1929 class of pilots training at Netheravon; it's possible that one of these young men encountered the ghost pilot trapped there after his untimely death while training for combat in World War I.

"Hey!" the pilot shouted at the mysterious shadow figure. "Can you hear me? Hey! What do you want?"

The ghost made no sign of understanding, but his shoulders sagged noticeably, and moments later, he simply faded from sight. The form blew away like smoke on a breeze, and as it did the barracks returned to normal. Within a few heartbeats, the beds had once again filled with men sleeping soundly, each of them blissfully unaware of their brush with the paranormal. The pilot was relieved at the reappearance of his friends, but sleep eluded him for the rest of the night. His mind lingered on the ghostly visitor, which he decided had to have been the soul of a fellow pilot who had died during the war but for some reason could not rest easy. In fact, the young man never again enjoyed a truly restful night's sleep during the remainder of his Netheravon posting. Every night he tossed and turned, praying for sleep yet afraid of what would happen if he did nod off, always half-expecting to be revisited by the ominous spirit of that deceased Great War aviator.

That encounter was just the first of many with the spectral pilot of Netheravon, who we can probably safely assume perished in a training accident during World War I. In the years after the initial episode, witnesses began reporting a figure dressed in Royal Flying Corp pilot's gear silently wandering the darkened barracks during the wee hours of the night. The apparition was seen on the grounds outside as well, neck craned, looking up to the moonlit sky. He cut a distant, lonely figure. Pilots began to believe that seeing him was bad luck and foretold impending doom.

The outbreak of World War II in 1939 accelerated the need for pilots once more, and the Flying Training School was kept busy. Thousands of young men arrived to undertake the training that the tragic ghost had not been able to complete during the conflict a generation earlier, and as their numbers swelled, sightings of the ethereal figure increased as well.

One such trainee was 18-year-old airman Alan C. Wood. Wood was allocated a barrack bed space in one of the old World War I–era wooden huts on the edge of the airfield. Ten other men were billeted in the same barrack, all about the same age. During his time at Netheravon, Wood had an encounter with the airfield's supernatural resident. The experience so profoundly affected him that it led to a lifelong interest in ghosts and the occult, jumpstarting more than 60 years of research into eerie stories from across Britain. Wood, it should be mentioned, spent 24 years in the military and another 31 years as a police officer—a serious-minded man, he approached his research in a matter-of-fact manner with a trained eye for detail and accuracy. His testimony, therefore, should be viewed with a great deal of credence.

"One night, I was fast asleep in my bed, when I awoke for no reason," Wood writes in his book, *Military Ghosts*. "The room was dark, but with night vision it was easy to see the whole room without turning on the lights. Standing at the bottom of my bed was a dark figure dressed in First World War flying clothing of a primitive nature. I sat up in the bed and stared at the figure. It did not move. I was not afraid. Being young, fit and unafraid of anything

I roared expletives at the figure, which, perhaps startled by my aggressive behaviour, moved and faded away!"

Wood's yelling echoed loudly in the barracks, startling the other young airmen from their sleep. Bleary-eyed and groggy, they jumped from their beds. What the bloody hell was going on, they demanded. Wood, rather sheepishly, told his mates that he had seen a ghost. To a man, they were furious. They had thought that Wood was in some kind of trouble, or that perhaps a sergeant was ordering them from bed for a surprise inspection or training exercise, or, worst of all, that it might have been a German attack on the airfield. To learn their sleep had been interrupted because Wood had supposedly seen a ghost—a ghost, for blooming sake!—was simply too much. They hurled any number of colourful insults and threats at Wood and then returned to their cots. Wood, more embarrassed than frightened by the whole episode, lay back in his bed, rolled onto his side and fell asleep.

Wood was able to put the episode behind him pretty quickly, but he never forgot it, and he spent decades trying to come to grips with what he had seen. He chronicled in his writing the personal sightings of many others at Netheravon, perhaps taking comfort in the knowledge that he wasn't alone in his experience.

After World War II, use of Netheravon as an airfield declined so that by the 1950s, it was no longer used for pilot training but had become instead a training centre for the RAF Police. Ghostly sightings and other unusual phenomena continued. During this period, a canine officer posted to Netheravon reported that his dog, an otherwise fearless German shepherd, suddenly and inexplicably grew frightened during a routine nighttime patrol of the air base. It was well into the patrol when the dog suddenly began cowering behind its handler's legs and whimpering like a terrified puppy. There was nothing present that should have unnerved the dog—nothing visible, at any rate—but the officer did notice something in the air that caused his own skin to crawl. It was just a feeling, a heaviness in the air that made him ill at ease. Neither man nor dog had any interest in remaining in that location, and they hurriedly left.

In 1963, the RAF left Netheravon completely. But the base would not sit empty for long. In 1966, the Army Air Corps took over Netheravon as an airfield for operating helicopters. It remains today the home of 7 Regiment Army Air Corps, whose main role is to provide liaison flying for the Regular Army and general aviation support for the Territorial Army.

Netheravon is also still reputed to be home to the spectral First World War pilot. There have been recent sightings of the resident ghost, a tragic young man who died a century ago and wasted away into nothing but shadow. Some say they feel his presence even when he chooses not to reveal himself. Although the RAF has moved on, this spectre continues to linger at the site of his untimely death, longing for the life that the Great War took from him.

The Ghostly Cavalry of Neuve Eglise

A squadron of proud German cavalry emerges from the cover of a small forest, their lances held aloft, bright sun gleaming off the steel blades. One hundred horses line up along the crest of the hill, looking out upon the small village of Neuve Eglise in the distance and the squadron of French cavalry that stands between them and the tiny hamlet.

Spotting the enemy emerging from the forest, a French officer rides out before his mounted troops and forms them into a long line. He intends to give battle this day, and God willing, drive away the hated "Hun." When at last he is satisfied his men and their mounts are in good order, he draws his sword, stretching out his sabre toward the German *uhlans*, and urges his mount to surge forward. The whole line takes off with him, swords high, gathering pace, grim determination etched on every face. Horses snort and whinny, their hides soon shining with sweat. The sound of pounding hooves carries across the fields and down to the sleepy village of Neuve Eglise, alerting the villagers to the battle about to unfold nearby.

The opposing cavalry crash into one another. Swords slash at the enemy, lances are driven through wool and flesh, and weapons and their wielders alike are splashed with blood. Troops tumble from their saddles and are trampled by hooves. Men shout and horses scream. Soon the French begin to break off in a panicked race for survival. For them, now, it is flight or capture. Fallen soldiers lie about the ground like toy soldiers tipped from the box. The triumphant German soldiers erupt in a chorus of cheers.

Then, just as quickly as the skirmish ends, the horses and their riders fade from view. The dead and dying troops disappear from the field. It's as if the battle never even occurred. But it did happen—sometime during the early days of World War I—and has continued to be fought over and over again in an endless loop of violence and death ever since, on certain mournful days when an oppressive discomfort settles over the valley.

Long after the rifles and artillery fell silent, long after men stopped dying in the muddy trenches of France, the ghosts of war remain on many First World War battlefields. The woods and fields outside Neuve Eglise in the Aire-sur-la-Lys region is one such haunted location. The wounds of an unnamed encounter that took place there, just one of thousands of barely recorded skirmishes fought during the Great War, have not yet healed despite the passage of so many years. French and German cavalry are locked in an eternal cycle of dying so that while memories of the original skirmish are all but gone, its ghostly legend lingers to this day.

Aire-sur-la-Lys, located in northwestern France near the Belgian border, has long been fought over by France and her neighbours. In the Middle Ages, the then-independent Burgundy contested possession of the region with France. Later, the Spanish fought for its control, claiming it should rightfully belong to the Spanish Netherlands. Then, in the Franco-Prussian War of 1870–1871, French and German armies clashed there. Aire-sur-la-Lys has been fought over on numerous occasions over hundreds of years, and its soil is deeply soaked with blood.

The Great War carried on that tradition of bloodshed. French and British armies paid dearly as they fought Germany for mastery of the region, launching wave after wave of infantry against the enemy in numerous battles that saw thousands of men die for gains of mere metres. The deep mud, miserable weather and catastrophic casualties made this region one of the most hellish sectors of the Western Front.

Finally, after more than four long years of fighting and death, in the grey November of 1918, the guns of World War I fell silent. An eerie stillness descended upon the battlefields where thousands of dead lay unburied in sodden trenches, many of them never to be identified. Northern France was a dismal expanse of shattered villages and towns that had been reduced to rubble. The land was a barren moonscape of bomb craters and skeletal trees. Starving, shell-shocked refugees clogged the roads. Millions of soldiers—British, Canadian, American, French and others—sullenly awaited the day when they would be demobilized and could leave this hell. The war was over, but the misery certainly had not ended.

Perhaps even the dead were ill at ease during that dreary winter. Certainly James Wentworth Day, a young British soldier who would later go on to become a famous writer and broadcaster, believed this to be the case. A disturbing wartime experience convinced him that the soldiers who had fallen in battle were not resting peacefully in their graves and were tragically doomed to continue to fight the terrible war. The episode profoundly affected Wentworth Day, shaping his beliefs and even his career.

The day in which his hair-raising experience took place began like any other. Early that winter morning, Wentworth Day, accompanied by a friend, Corporal Barr, left his unit's encampment to pick up mail and rations from a distant depot. Hours later, having gathered the food—sadly, more tinned beef and hardened loaves of bread—and picked up letters and parcels from home, the two men started back to camp. It was about 3:30 in the afternoon. Being early winter, the sun was already slowly sliding from the sky. It wasn't yet dark, but shadows were stretching across the landscape.

Not far along the road was a birch forest atop a knot of hills, its trees torn and twisted into grotesque shapes by shell blasts. The shattered woods were yet another reminder of the destruction of war. Suddenly, movement in the forest caught the soldiers' attention.

The two men watched in stunned silence as German cavalry swept out from among those skeletal trees, a dozen or more *uhlans*, wearing, in Wentworth Day's own words, "those queer high-topped hats which they had worn in the dead days of 1914." Instinctively, Wentworth Day and Barr reached for their rifles. Although greatly outnumbered, the men prepared to fight for their lives. Relief flooded over them when, moments later, they saw a force of French dragoons appear in the valley ahead. Evidently spying the enemy, the French cavalry spurred their horses into a gallop and raced up the slope toward the Germans. At the same time, the German cavalry sprang into motion, surging downhill in a seemingly unstoppable wave. It was a marvellous sight: the French dragoons in their brass cuirasses, sabres held aloft over their heads, plumes dancing from their helmets, racing to fight the German cavalry whose men, in their pristine uniforms and high, four-cornered caps, charged with lances levelled.

But there was no clash of mounted men. Just as the opposing forces were about to collide, the men and their mounts faded from view. There was no sign of them. It was if they had never been there. All that remained in the orange glow of the setting sun was an empty field, the shattered wood and a small village in the near distance.

"Did you see that?" Wentworth Day asked, his voice a hoarse whisper.

Barr, who looked white and uneasy, nodded feebly. "Aye, something mighty queer," he said.

Both men were shaken by the seeming impossibility of what they had just seen. Their hearts pounded in their chests, and their mouths went dry. Stunned speechless by the ghostly spectacle, neither man spoke for the remainder of the drive back to camp. Even as the evening advanced and the shock began to wear off, both men were reluctant to speak. Finally, however, in hushed tones so no one could overhear, they compared their experiences and shared their thoughts. Both men had seen the exact same drama play out. Both were left with the same questions. In an attempt to find some answers, and in the absence of other duties, they decided that they would return to the site of the phenomenon the following morning.

As agreed, the next morning, Wentworth Day and Barr headed out for Neuve Eglise. It was a "skeleton of a village,"

Wentworth Day recalled, in which most of the buildings had collapsed, piles of rubble littered the streets and tough-looking weeds filled what were once well-tended yards. The few villagers who remained appeared despondent and desperate, their faces sallow with malnutrition and their eyes ringed dark from years of fear and worry. Wentworth Day approached an aged villager shuffling on uncertain legs through the ruins of his community, his creased face reflecting the many years he had lived and the sadness of his life. Wentworth Day related the experience of the day before and asked about the haunted woods, then watched as the old man nodded thoughtfully.

"Ah! Monsieur, that wood is a very sad wood, you know," the old villager explained. "It is on the frontier... a wood of dead men! In the wars of Napoleon, in the war of 1870, in this last war... the cavalry of France and Germany have always met each other by that wood, and many men have fallen in battle."

A crooked, bony hand reached out to grab Wentworth Day's arm. "Come, I show you." Gently pulling the soldier along, the old man picked his way around shell holes and piles of rubble. Wheezing with the exertion, he stopped in front of a tiny churchyard surrounded by a rickety wooden fence. Aged headstones poked up through the earth, some so old moss grew in the faded inscriptions. Pushing through the gate, the old man stepped into the cemetery and pointed toward a number of fresh graves in one corner. There were buried the dead from the cavalry skirmish that had taken place nearby just a few years earlier. The villagers had retrieved the bodies from the battlefield and given them a suitable funeral, regardless of their nationality. Nearby were older gravesites belonging to soldiers who had fallen in the vicinity during the Franco-Prussian and Napoleonic wars.

First witnessing a battle fought by spectral soldiers and then solemnly visiting their graves left a lasting impression on Wentworth Day. He became a lifelong believer in the paranormal and dedicated much of his life to researching and writing about hauntings and other supernatural phenomena. He became one of the best-known "ghost-hunters" of mid-20th–century Britain.

The blood spilled during several wars caused the woods outside Neuve Eglise to become frightfully haunted. Even before the Great War, villagers had long reported weird lights and mysterious sounds, including constant shrieks and howls that caused blood to curdle and which could not be explained. Then, in the aftermath of the First World War, the sadness and death that clung to the woods began to coalesce into the ghosts of the most recent French and German cavalrymen to die there. The ghostly horsemen patrol the woods and fields, clashing when the apparitions stumble upon one another. Even when you don't see them, you may hear them; the hoof beats of invisible horses can be heard thundering down roads and across fields, while the agonizing screams of the wounded and dying rend the air.

Although tragic and occasionally frightening, the spectral vestiges of the brief but bloody battle on the outskirts of Neuve Eglise have managed to keep this forgotten and unnamed Great War clash alive. In particular, the spectral skirmishing serves as a lasting reminder of the tragedy of war and how few problems are ever truly resolved by force of arms. Those soldiers, like Neuve Eglise itself, exist in a border region—on one side is the mortal realm belonging to the living, and on the other is the afterlife where the dead reside. They no longer belong to the former, but as long as they continue to fight, they will never rest peacefully in the latter. Will these soldiers ever realize the war is over, and that traditional enemies France and Germany are now partners in a 21st-century Europe? Or are they doomed to continue their combat forever?

Heartache at the Prince of Wales Hotel

With its historical streets, charming shops and romantic inns, Niagara-on-the-Lake, Ontario, lures vacationers who are in search of respite and relaxation. The town is one of the province's most popular tourist destinations. But in this historic community, ghosts from the past roam the streets on equal footing with the tourists, earning Niagara-on-the-Lake the title of Ontario's spectral capital.

One of the most haunted locations in Niagara-on-the-Lake is also one of the most beautiful. The elegant, majestic Prince of Wales Hotel is among the best hotels in all of Canada, a property noted for its refined accommodations, spot-on traditional high tea service, fine dining and world-class spa. The Prince of Wales also has a long tradition of hauntings that mark the building as a hotspot for paranormal activity.

While tragic, blood-soaked battlefields, mournful graves and ancient ruins are most often associated with ghosts (and certainly Niagara-on-the-Lake has its share of these), in truth any building or landscape has the potential to host lost souls wandering the land of the living. The Prince of Wales Hotel is far from the Hollywood depiction of a haunted building, yet it is haunted just the same.

Just as the Prince of Wales stands out from the other fine hotels in Niagara-on-the-Lake by virtue of its splendour, so too does its ghost story prove distinctive from the many others in town. Whereas a great many of the spectral residents trace their restlessness back to the War of 1812, during which Niagara-on-the-Lake (then known as Newark) was fought over on several occasions and burned by American invaders, the female apparition that calls the Prince of Wales home is of more recent vintage, dating to World War I. And, perhaps befitting a property of such beauty, this haunting tale is at its heart a love story—a tragic one, to be sure, but a love story nonetheless.

The story centres upon an eternally mournful female ghost whose love was so intense that it survived not only her beloved's death but her own as well, and it keeps her bound to the hotel where the ill-fated couple spent their final tearful moments together. The melancholy ghost glides through the richly wooded hallways, her ethereal skirt brushing over the floor, and her mind relives cherished moments with her husband as she faithfully awaits his now decades overdue return. She refuses to give up her vigil, convinced they will be together again if only she remains patient and waits a little while longer. But a reunion is never to be. The woman's tireless devotion and obvious suffering tug at the heartstrings of all the hotel staff and guests who encounter her. And make no mistake, the list of those who have experienced paranormal activity at the Prince of Wales Hotel is lengthy enough to fill a good-sized registry.

Sometimes the spirit appears to be of flesh and blood, dressed in period clothing but otherwise indistinguishable from the other guests staying at the hotel. Many witnesses mistake her for someone in costume, which is hardly an unusual sight in a community so full of museums and historic tours. It's only when the woman fades away or walks through a wall that they realize there is something unusual about her. Other times, she appears as a vague and somewhat hazy reflection of her old self. In either case, the spectral woman is stunningly beautiful, but her angelic features are shadowed by great sadness. She wanders the halls aimlessly, oblivious to those sharing the hotel with her and to the luxurious surroundings. Guests can't help but notice her tears and wonder how she could be so upset in such a beautiful place. Who is this woman, they ask themselves, and what is her connection to the Prince of Wales?

Her story doesn't begin with sadness. Just the opposite, it begins with the euphoria that only true love can bring. It was during the early days of World War I that a young woman fell hopelessly in love with a soldier training for overseas duty at nearby Camp Niagara. What started as a friendship quickly became something more intimate. They were young and in love; days were spent in passionate bliss, and evenings were filled with dreams for their future.

The woman who now haunts the Prince of Wales Hotel had only a few blissful weeks with her lover while he was a soldier training at Camp Niagara.

But a dark cloud hovered over their courtship; the woman knew that her beloved would soon be pulled from her arms to fight in a war that seemed, to her young mind, senseless and so very far away. When she thought about his coming absence her heart would ache, so she chose not to focus on their eventual parting but instead attempted to cherish the short time they had together. As the day of his departure drew near, the lovers made a quick decision: they would marry so that when he was overseas, they would be together in matrimony if not in person. Somehow, it just felt right.

The Prince of Wales was selected as both the venue for the ceremony and the honeymoon destination. Circumstances dictated that the soldier could not provide his bride with the kind of wedding most young girls dream of while growing up, but he was determined she would have some luxury on her special day. The honeymoon was just a few short days of leave, but they were determined to make the most of it.

The night before the young soldier was to board a train for Halifax, where he would board a ship to be transported to the killing fields of France, the lovers said a tearful farewell. He promised he would return to her after the war, while she vowed to remain true to him and wait faithfully until they were together once more. She swore she would wait until eternity, if need be. Her oath, while likely not intended to be literal, would prove to be sadly prophetic.

True to her word, even as the months of waiting turned into a year, the young woman remained desperately in love. She wrote letters daily and spent much of her free time imagining the happy reunion. Not for a moment did she entertain the possibility that her husband may not return; she was convinced their love would see him through any danger.

So when news arrived that her husband had been killed, she simply refused to believe it. It was impossible. He had promised to return to her. He promised. This was some kind of mistake, she convinced herself, a tragic mis-understanding. He would return. And so she patiently waited, convinced he would be found alive—perhaps in a German hospital or prison camp.

Most of her time was spent in her room in the hotel, alone with cherished memories of the man she loved, reading and rereading his letters now stained by her tears. The people of Niagara-on-the-Lake became accustomed to seeing her sad, expectant face staring out at tree-lined Picton Street between slightly parted curtains. Guests in the hotel frequently had their rest disturbed by the sounds of sorrowful sobs late at night as she cried herself to sleep.

But as months turned into years, the woman grew thinner and quieter, withdrawing almost completely into an inner world where she relived moments spent with her beloved. Soon she couldn't bear to leave her room, and in time she died of a broken heart, a photo of her husband clutched firmly in her hand. She had perished believing to the end that her husband would one day come back to her.

Sadly, steadfast reluctance to give up her vigil trans-formed her into a disembodied spirit. This spectral echo of her former self is bound to the Prince of Wales Hotel by the promise made a century earlier to faithfully await her husband's return. Sadly, the ghost's dream of being reunited with her loved one can never be realized. Her melancholy mood prevents her from enjoying the charm of her surroundings. Her stay is not one of relaxation and pleasure, as it is with mortal guests, but rather an enduring torment from which there seems to be no escape.

The spectral woman is felt most often in the elegant main lobby, and on at least one occasion, guests were greeted upon their arrival by the sight of a beautiful but ethereal woman wearing an outdated, floor-length dress wandering past the reception desk. She is also said to frequent room 307, or to linger in the bar, sitting comfortably in a cushioned chair, oblivious to the world around her. Some passersby have even seen her ghostly image peering out a window onto the street, as if waiting to see her husband come walking up the road.

One vacationing woman had her sleep disturbed by this spectral woman. It was late into the night, and she and her husband were sound asleep after a day of exploring the Niagara sights when the bed began to shake, as if someone was trying to wake the sleeping pair. The motion startled the woman from her sleep. She looked over to her husband, thinking he had been the one to wake her, but his soft snoring told her he was still soundly asleep. Deciding she had dreamed the sensation, the woman returned her head to the pillow and quickly dozed off.

It wasn't long before a determined shaking woke her again. Again, her husband was still asleep, and again, she convinced herself she had imagined the whole thing. Back to sleep she went. Then it happened again. But this time, it was different. In addition to the insistent shaking, the groggy woman felt cold hands under the blankets and saw the face of a youthful woman leaning over the bed, staring right at her—no body, just a face. The apparition didn't linger long, but, now wide awake, the woman was too afraid to go back to sleep and spent the rest of the night peering into the darkened recesses of the room, looking for the mysterious entity that had disturbed her.

Was the ghost upset by a couple enjoying each other's company in her domain? After all, she longs to feel the arms of her husband wrapped around her once more, so perhaps companionship in any form, even something as simple as a man and woman sleeping contentedly side by side, causes her pain and anguish, even jealousy.

Sightings of the spectral woman are rare, but her antics are not. She tends to make her presence known at night in various subtle ways: following staff around with disembodied footsteps, playfully moving objects and even lightly rapping on patron's doors. For a former staff member, a skeptic at first, a single inexplicable event was enough to make her a believer in the paranormal. She was at the front desk when she heard her name being called out by a woman's voice. The voice sounded as if it had come from behind her, but when the clerk turned around, no one was there. It was evening; the lobby was quiet, and there were no guests or staff around. How does one explain the voice rationally? This staff member couldn't. Nor could she explain the sudden unease she felt, as if she was being watched. In that instant, she knew ghosts truly existed and that the Prince of Wales lives up to its haunted reputation.

Shane Howard, formerly an employee at the Prince of Wales, had an experience there in the winter of 1999 that left him bewildered and shaken. Even now, years later, he struggles to make sense of that evening's events.

"I was working a shift from 3:00 to 11:00 PM, and Ms. Lai, the owner, was in the dining room with a few personal guests. Later in the evening she asked me to show them a guest room, so I went up to room 307—the room with a balcony overlooking the road—to turn the lights on and ensure it looked perfect," Shane recalls of that night. "When I came down from the room in the elevator, Ms. Lai and her guests were there waiting for me to take them up to the room. It was no more than three minutes later. We entered the suite and went into the bedroom. The lamp next to the bed was turned off (the light bulb didn't just burn out, as I turned the light back on and it worked fine), and the chair from the desk by the bed had been moved over about four feet nearer to the bed. Since I was in the room just minutes prior, I would have noticed both of these things. Ms. Lai and I both looked at each other and thought this was a little spooky."

Shane knew that he had left the room in ideal condition and that no other staff member would pull such a prank, especially when those being shown the room, wealthy businessmen representing potential clients, were guests of the owner. Shane also knew that the room was well known for its haunted activity and that people entering the room often become aware of a strong unseen presence. He's convinced that the mischievous individual that put the room in disarray was otherworldly in origin, perhaps letting the staff of the Prince of Wales know that room 307 is hers until such time as she chooses to check out. The experience didn't frighten Shane, but it did change him forever. Previously a skeptic, he now believes ghosts exist.

Although the hotel's ghost has traditionally avoided the basement, extensive renovations and remodelling a few years back seem to have disturbed the spirit, agitating her into activity. Soon after the work to transform the Secret Gardens Spa into one of Canada's best was completed, the ghost began occasionally to make her way downstairs to make her presence felt. A spa treatment usually involves soothing music, a tranquil setting and absolutely no excitement, but this is not always the case at the Prince of Wales. Sometimes, strange things happen to add just a touch of excitement. Maria herself can vouch for it.

One day in the winter of 2011 found Maria with her feet soaking for a relaxing pedicure. The beautician asked if she was in Niagara for a special occasion or simply a getaway. Maria replied neither, and explained that she was a freelance writer doing research for a travel article on the Prince of Wales Hotel. The spa treatment was just an unexpected but welcome perk. The conversation soon led into the various books Maria had written, and she mentioned one of our releases, *Ghosts of Niagara on-the-Lake*.

"Wow! I read that book cover to cover!" another beautician excitedly said. She proceeded to share how the hotel's lost spirit had recently become active in the spa; all manner of unusual phenomena had been experienced in the spa facilities, none of which had rational explanations. For example, foot soakers would randomly turn on and off. Beauticians would get one ready for a client and turn the jets on, only to find that they had shut off on their own moments later. On several occasions the staff called in servicemen to look into the foot baths, and each time, they were told there was absolutely nothing wrong with the units.

More incredibly, spa staff discovered that the spirit could—and would—communicate by turning the jets on in response to questions. Maria found this assertion too improbable to believe, but she decided to play along when the beauticians suggested she try.

"If you are here, please turn on the water," Maria said aloud, addressing the ghost. To her complete surprise, the foot tub started running on its own. She couldn't believe what had just happened, and the wide eyes of the beauticians told her they were amazed as well.

They turned off the jets, and Maria proceeded to ask a host of other yes or no questions. Not only would the water turn on by itself whenever the answer was affirmative, but the ghost also always answered correctly, even when obscure historical questions were posed. Interestingly, when asked if she liked the recent renovations done to the spa, nothing happened. Perhaps the construction had interrupted her peaceful vigil, or maybe she simply doesn't like change.

The ethereal woman has also been seen elsewhere in the Prince of Wales' basement since the renovations, floating silently through rooms and walls, obvious to how her sudden appearances disrupt the tranquility of the setting. A chill breeze will sometimes brush past someone, and quiet, sorrowful sobbing has been heard. Nowhere in the hotel is off limits to the apparition. The whole building—basement to attic—is her domain.

Driven by all-encompassing loyalty and love, the ghostly woman refuses to release her hold on the mortal world. She devotedly awaits the return of her beloved, but her vigil is destined to be an eternal one; her husband lies somewhere in an unmarked grave in France. And so she remains lonely, heartbroken and mournful to this day.

Ironically, the only thing keeping the lovers apart is this blind devotion. If the ghostly woman would only let go, her spirit would pass from the realm of the living and be reunited with her beloved on the other side, where he no doubt waits for her as faithfully as she does him.

The Great War cost millions of lives and severed countless relationships. The heart-wrenching tale of the lovelorn soul at the Prince of Wales Hotel makes us realize that the women who were left behind as their men went off to fight suffered as well. Those who lost husbands, sweethearts or sons were more casualties of the war, suffering emotional wounds that might scar over but never truly heal. It leads one to question: how many other women who lost loved ones were in death transformed by sorrow and heartbreak into restless spirits?

The Phantom Invasion of 1915

On the night of February 14, 1915, residents of Eastern Ontario settled into their beds. Pulling blankets up under their noses and ignoring the eerie sounds of chill winds rattling window frames and tree branches scratching at walls, thousands of people willed the cold away and awaited sleep. Some had managed to drift off, and many others were still restlessly tossing and turning, when sounds of alarm erupted from outside. Strange lights—flashing on and off, travelling at high speed, and accompanied by a mysterious sound like that of windmill blades cutting through the air—had appeared in the darkness overhead.

Similar scenes were being played out in several communities across Eastern Ontario, including the nation's capital, Ottawa. As frightened people stumbled from their homes to stare incredulously into the night sky, many worried that somehow Germany—though an ocean away—had found a way to send aircraft over Canada. Residents of these communities were on the verge of panic. When would the bombs begin to fall?

Soon, thanks to media coverage, the fear spread even farther. Newspaper headlines across the country the following morning captured the sense of dread felt by the people of Eastern Ontario the night before. The *Toronto Globe* on February 15, 1915, read, "Ottawa in darkness awaits aeroplane raid." Below that startling headline, the paper warned, "Several aeroplanes make a raid into the Dominion of Canada," and notified readers that "entire city of Ottawa in darkness, fearing bomb droppers." Another alarming article told readers that "machines crossed St. Lawrence River, passing over Brockville—two over Gananoque—seen by many citizens, heading for the capital—one was equipped with powerful searchlights—fire balls dropped."

For a nation already at war and reeling from the daily news of horrifying casualties among its young men fighting in France, these reports were terrifying. Nerves were stretched nearly to the breaking point. It appeared the grim realities of war were about to come home to Canada.

The so-called Phantom Invasion of 1915 is among the best and most widely documented cases of UFO sightings in Canadian history. It isn't just the startling nature of the eyewitness accounts that causes this episode to stand out, but also the sheer number of people who witnessed the unexplained lights, including several prominent members of society. In addition, the extreme detail with which these individuals reported their experiences adds a sense of credibility lacking in many UFO cases and serves to make this episode truly compelling. Also consider that the incident took place decades before the UFO phenomenon became part of popular consciousness. In 1915, there simply was no tradition of unidentified flying objects—nothing with which to fuel one's imagination.

The excitement began on February 14, 1915, around 9:15 PM, when the evening quiet in Brockville was interrupted by startled cries from along the waterfront. Fearing a fire or worse, people hastily threw coats on against the cold and raced down to the bank of the St. Lawrence River, from where the frightened cries had originated. There, dozens, perhaps hundreds of wide-eyed citizens watched in amazement as the lights of unidentified objects approached from across the river. The mysterious lights passed overhead with the "unmistakable sounds of the whirring motor" and then disappeared into the distance, headed north in the direction of Ottawa. This was no hysterical rabble or crowd of attention-seekers or drunken louts; among the throng were numerous respected businessmen, three town constables and the mayor.

About five minutes after these "mysterious aircraft" had passed overhead and were swallowed up by the night, the distinctive sound of another flying machine was heard echoing across the water, apparently originating near Morristown, New York, on the opposite bank of the St. Lawrence. With each passing second the noise became louder, and then lights, which appeared as mere pinpricks on the horizon, grew to become bright orbs. It soon became obvious that this mysterious craft would also fly over Brockville.

As it approached the town, the flying machine dropped three balls of fire into the river not far offshore. People began to panic. Some were convinced the fireballs were bombs dropped prematurely, perhaps incendiaries designed to burn towns to the ground. Others worried the fireballs could have been flares designed to help enemy pilots navigate in the darkness, marking the way for German bombers coming over the U.S. border or even across the vast expanse of the Atlantic Ocean. There were reports, including from Brockville's Mayor Donaldson himself, that suggested a beam of a bright light, like a searchlight, flashed out from the aircraft to light up an entire city block.

A few minutes later, another aerial invader was reported to have passed over the east end of town, and then yet another was seen crossing over the river to the west of Brockville. The mayor of nearby Gananoque, a village located southwest of Brockville, called Mayor Donaldson and breathlessly reported that in his own community, two UFOs had been distinctly heard passing overhead, though in their case there were no accompanying lights.

All told, there were reports of as many as half a dozen unidentified, possibly hostile aircraft flying over Eastern Ontario. To Mayor Donaldson, it appeared Canada was under attack. While the people of his town fretted, he had duties to perform. First, he ordered the police chief to reassure his citizens that they were safe and were instructed, above all, to maintain order. Then, he reached for the telephone and called the office of the Prime Minister, Sir Robert Borden, "to advise him that unidentified aircraft were seen crossing over Brockville from across the St. Lawrence in the direction of Ottawa."

With a possible threat near at hand, Borden held an immediate meeting with his cabinet and senior members of the military. After reviewing the reports that had filtered through from Brockville and Gananoque about the mysterious flyers, all who were present agreed the threat seemed credible and imminent. The Commissioner of the Dominion Police and commanding officers of local militia units were notified of the danger and their forces called out. There was concern that the lights of Parliament Hill, shining like a beacon in the night, would make an easy target for aerial bombers, so they were ordered turned off.

Parliament Hill went dark at about 11:15 PM, and the entire city of Ottawa followed suit about five minutes later. Shutters were secured, and windows were darkened throughout the capital region. Military and police marksmen clambered to the roofs of government buildings in Ottawa under orders to shoot down any hostile aircraft, though surely all involved realized that if indeed the aircraft were hostile, the rifles carried by these soldiers and policemen would offer no real defence. Still, something had to be done, if for no other reason than to reassure the fearful populace.

This was the first black-out and air raid threat in Canadian history, and it came only one month after the first air raid on Britain, wherein several people died and dozens of properties were damaged by bombs dropped from Zeppelins. Ottawa braced itself for the worst.

To everyone's relief, the attack never took place. No aircraft appeared overhead, and no bombs fell from the sky to wreak havoc upon the defenceless city. With the arrival of dawn, people who had huddled fearfully in their homes all night tentatively emerged onto the streets and craned their necks. The skies were empty. The danger had passed. And yet many people in Ottawa, to say nothing of Brockville and Gananoque, were shaken for quite a while afterward. The entire episode was beyond comprehension.

But this was no isolated incident. Eastern Ontario was not the only location to experience UFO activity that night. Shortly after midnight, several people in Richmond Hill, a town just north of Toronto, notified local police of a "strange aeroplane" that had hovered menacingly over their homes. The noiseless object seemed to be suspended in the sky, intimidating in its silence. After several minutes, it flew away. Elsewhere, in the hills of Caledon not far to the west, many residents reported seeing a number of mysterious white-blue flashes in the night sky for which no explanation could be found.

Later, a man in Guelph saw "three moving lights passing over the agricultural college." Fear mixed with curiosity as he watched them first hover above the building, then dart back and forth over the property before once again settling into a hover. The man awoke other tenants of the boarding house in which he was staying, and together a dozen or so bewitched people watched the silent lights until dawn.

Meanwhile, much farther to the west in rural Manitoba, three men were returning home from a late night of curling in Morden when they heard a strange sound in the sky. Pulling up the reins of the wagon in which they were riding, the men looked up to see a bright light pass overhead, moving to the northwest. They watched wide-eyed as it disappeared over the horizon. When asked by a newspaper reporter to describe what they had seen, all indicated that it had been an "aeroplane" travelling swiftly through the sky.

It seemed that all across Central Canada, mysterious aircraft had made unexplained nighttime flights. Interestingly, the UFOs as described by witnesses did not operate within the parameters of the primitive airplanes of the day. No flying machine, except for a gas-filled Zeppelin, could hover motionlessly as some witnesses reported the mysterious craft were capable of. But Zeppelins were lumbering whales, slow and ungainly. They were incapable of the rapid, agile flight these UFOs had demonstrated. Indeed, even the faster fighter planes of the day would have been easily outpaced by these mysterious aircraft. Additionally, it should be noted that nighttime flying was in its infancy owing to primitive navigational instrumentation, and was therefore something few pilots would risk. In short, heads across the nation were being scratched in the days following the Phantom Invasion. Just what had these UFOs been? Soon, an unexpected—and, in retrospect, unlikely—explanation emerged.

Word came out that the panic in Eastern Ontario might have been the handiwork of pranksters in Morristown, New York. Supposedly, three balloons with fireworks dangling below were sent aloft on the night of February 14 in celebration of the 100th anniversary of the end of the War of 1812. The fireworks, so the rational explanation goes, created the impression of aircraft lights and falling balls of fire.

Officials in Ottawa and the residents of Brockville and Gananoque refused to believe this story. To them, it seemed highly improbable. Nonetheless, an investigation was launched to determine whether there was any truth to it. On the morning of February 15, Constable Storey of the Brockville Police Department is said to have found the remains of a paper balloon near Eastern Hospital, and soon after, a second paper balloon was found in eastern Brockville along the riverbank. These discoveries seemed to validate the explanation provided by American authorities. It wasn't long before news began to spread across telegraph lines that the whole episode had been nothing more than a harmless hoax, and the tension lifted. People were able to laugh at how they, the morning papers and politicians alike had been duped by a few youthful pranksters with toy balloons. Ottawa officially passed off the incident as a case of nerves frayed thin by the war—a mass hysteria within the town of Brockville.

However, many people then and in the years since were not so sure. Of the many onlookers that night who had distinctly seen the objects pass overhead and disappear into the distance, no one had seen even one, let alone two, of those lights drop from the sky within the boundary of their community. Moreover, the number of lanterns sent aloft doesn't mesh with the number of objects seen that night. And what of the spotlight-like beam seen in Brockville by none other than the town's mayor, or the distinctive sound of engines in the skies above? Balloons can't explain them. And just how long could a firework carried aloft on the wind burn for, anyway? Supporting the views of naysayers was the official report of the generally sceptical *Dominion Observatory*, which publicly rejected the explanation being offered. The *Observatory* noted that the prevailing winds for the night of February 14/15 were from the east and would not have taken the balloons north toward Ottawa from Brockville.

Adding to the weight of mounting evidence against the UFOs being balloons were the accounts reported elsewhere across Canada, before news of the invasion of Eastern Ontario had made the papers. How can one discount all of these as well? The answer is simple: one can't. It's almost certain that the residents of Brockville, to say nothing of those in Gananoque, Guelph, Richmond Hill and Morden, Manitoba, had not mistaken paper balloons for something more ominous after all.

So what really happened? No one can say for certain who or what appeared in the sky over much of Central Canada that night in 1915, but what seems certain is that a massive cover-up took place immediately after, probably pushed upon Canadian authorities by the United States. Still neutral in the war, the American government may well have been worried that fear among American citizens of German aircraft operating above Canada—and therefore clearly capable of also striking the United States—might have led to hysteria that might have propelled the U.S. into the war. Or perhaps the Americans knew more than they cared to admit. Had the U.S. Army Air Corps been experimenting with some secret aircraft?

There may be an even stranger possibility. Some conspiracy theorists say that the democratic U.S. government has long been subverted by powerful groups within the nation allying themselves with alien forces. Had the mysterious flying objects witnessed that night been alien in origin?

Imagining UFO encounters is exciting, but for those who live through one it can be a traumatic, life changing experience. Add to that the fear of invasion by a wartime enemy, and one can easily see why the 1915 mass sighting is the most notorious in Canada's history. It would be hard to overstate the excitement generated by the startling incident, not just in the public and press, but also in the government. Since 1915, UFO reports across Canada have been endless—and endlessly fascinating. But none have yet compared to the Phantom Invasion in terms of drama, scale or sheer number of witnesses. Canada's first brush with UFOs remains its most compelling. To this day, UFO researchers debate the Phantom Invasion of 1915: a prank gone horribly wrong, or a true invasion of Canadian air space by mysterious aircraft of a possibly extraterrestrial nature?

The Spectres of Crécy

Colonel Shepheard jerked upright in bed. Icy fear gripped his heart. He listened, frozen with apprehension. Wind crept like ghostly fingers along the walls and upon the tile shingles overhead. But there was no other sound, nothing to suggest anything amiss. It was just a nightmare, he told himself. But his brain refused to accept it, and his heart continued to hammer like a drum against his chest. A seasoned army officer, Shepheard had been in battle on several occasions and had even grown hardened to its horrors, but he had never in his life been so frightened as in those moments in a darkened cottage in a quiet French village.

Although the full identity or even nationality of Colonel Shepheard has never been documented, his experience was recorded by paranormal researcher and Great War veteran James Wentworth Day, and subsequently has been passed down for decades. It remains, 100 years later, one of the most intriguing ghost stories to come from any soldier on the Western Front.

Colonel Shepheard was a staff officer during the First World War. One day saw him travelling by car across the French countryside from Hazebrouck to Wimereux on official business. He was accompanied by a French captain acting as an interpreter and aide. Having completed their business, the two men dined at Wimereux. By then, dark was fast approaching, so they decided to stay the night before departing early the next morning for their return to trip to Hazebrouck.

With the arrival of nightfall, the fields and woods outside the cottage in which the men were billeted came alive with the trilling of crickets. Standing at the window of his bedroom, Shepheard watched as fireflies in the trees and shrubs winked at him. The sky was clear, a black backdrop sprinkled with pinpricks of light and a half-moon surrounded by a hazy, prismatic ring. Despite the peaceful beauty of the scene, the colonel felt a dark melancholy settling over him. He badly missed his wife; he missed his country. But this was where he was needed, or so the powers that be said. He trusted their judgement, of course, but he longed to return home.

Feeling morose, Colonel Shepheard turned from the window and crawled into bed. The coarse, yellowed linen sheets were clean, and the open window ensured the room was well-aired, yet a faint musty smell lingered. He was restless, and sleep eluded him. Shepheard nodded off a few times, but each time, he awoke just a short while later. Something troubled him—something he couldn't explain but that had put his nerves on edge.

Finally, however, exhaustion took its toll, and he fell into a deep sleep. During the night, the colonel had an unusually detailed dream in which he was driving the same road again, in the same car and through the same villages. But this time, the car slowed down and stopped in one of the tiny, photogenic villages. It was an ancient collection of stone cottages huddled under the steeple of a medieval church. Something caught the colonel's eye. Ahead, through the morning mist, he glimpsed hooded, cloaked figures slowly rising up from the ground on either side of the road. There were hundreds of them, silent apparitions from some long-past era in history. Their cloaks were grey, almost luminous, with a fine, silvery bloom on them like moths' wings. They wore knee-length, padded garments with long sleeves, with helmets atop their wispy heads and ethereal swords hanging from their hips. Shepheard stared at those pale wraiths, unable to move. His eyes travelled to their faces, which were immobile, void of emotion and lifeless. Every one of them was staring fixedly at him. Then, slowly, they all sank back into the ground. A breath later, they were gone.

Waking with a start, Shepheard found himself trembling and sweating. Rising to get a drink of water from a nearby pitcher, he glanced out the window and noticed that clouds now stretched across the moon like dark shadows. The darkness was tense, filled with the deep sighing of leaves presaging a storm.

Colonel Shepheard struggled to return to sleep, and he awoke the next morning still shaken by his dream. It had felt more real, more detailed than any dream he had ever experienced before, and something about it unsettled him. He felt there was more to it than mere fantasy. After dressing, he joined his French aide at breakfast. Throughout the meal, his mind continued to wander back to that village, and he dined in silence. Finally, dishes were cleared. Above their heads, a ceiling fan churned the air while through the windows a warm summer breeze billowed the curtains. The two officers sat quietly at the table, sipping their tea.

Colonel Shepheard shifted uncomfortably in his chair and cleared his throat repeatedly, unsure how to proceed. He feared being ridiculed by his companion for bringing up a nightmare, but he desperately wanted answers, which perhaps the Frenchman could provide. Finally, he simply dove headlong into the subject. Shepheard opened up about his shocking dream of the night before, sharing every detail of the nightmare and his reaction to it. Far from ridiculing him, the French officer listened to the story without interruption. He nodded on occasion and seemed far less surprised than Shepheard had expected. It was almost, the colonel thought to himself, as if the Frenchman had heard this story before.

"Monsieur, can you describe that village where your car stopped in the dream?" the French officer asked when Shepheard had finished his story.

Colonel Shepheard said he could, and related with great precision the village he had seen twice: once in reality, and once in his dream.

The French officer nodded knowingly. "Ah. That makes sense. The village you saw in your dream, one of the villages we passed through yesterday, was Crécy. You have seen in your dream the English archers who fought, and perhaps died, on the Crécy battlefield in 1346."

Shepheard's mind raced to catch up with the revelation and tried to recall the history lessons of his youth. He remembered how on August 26, 1346, in the opening phases of the Hundred Years' War, King Edward III's English army of perhaps 10,000 men was brought to battle by a numerically superior French force, the size of which was between 30,000 and 70,000 men. The English bowmen had dug pits and lined the muddy fields with sharpened stakes to impede advancing cavalry. Despite these obstacles, the French knights charged and were cut down in the hundreds by longbow arrows. Over 1500 Frenchmen died, including the cream of the nobility, against only a few hundred English dead. King Edward was able to advance north and capture Calais. This battle was the decisive English victory at the outset of the war, helping create for the English an aura of invincibility and securing an empire on French soil. It was, in short, one of the most momentous battles in history, and Shepheard had witnessed—in his dream, at least—the spirits of those who had won it for England.

If you, like us, like your history mixed with a ghostly tale or two, you'll love Crécy. The battlefield is located literally just a couple hundred metres outside the town of Crécy, and the virtually level expanse of fields seems at odds with the historical accounts of French knights charging uphill. Once one climbs the observation tower, however, it becomes clear that the terrain is not as flat as it initially appears—and that any attacking force would have been dangerously exposed against bowmen capable of unleashing a hail of arrows at 1000 metres. These unremarkable fields were quite literally a killing ground.

Perhaps unsurprisingly, this scene of one of the bloodiest battles of the Middle Ages is also one of the most haunted attractions in France, home to ghosts of both nations. Colonel Shepheard is far from the only person to be startled by the paranormal at Crécy. Glowing orbs, eerie lights and full-body apparitions have been reported on the Crécy battlefield by people who live nearby and by others who visit the historical locale. If the sheer number of sightings is any indication, the spirits from the past want their stories told. They want the world to remember their stunning victory, and perhaps even the terrible cost of war.

It seems likely that the Crécy battlefield and witnesses themselves are experiencing what is known in parapsychology as a "place memory event," also known as a residual haunting. Such a haunting is considered a psychic memory of an event or of a human personality that simply replays itself over and over again like a tape recording. This type of event is triggered by some unknown force, though many parapsychologists theorize that various atmospheric conditions, such as a thunderstorm or a time of great humidity, may prompt such events.

Some people view Crécy as merely a hallowed battlefield, a reminder of one of history's pivotal events. Others believe it is alive with ghostly activity, the scene of eternal combat and deep emotional scars. Did the First World War dredge up latent emotions and long-dead combatants? For four years, British soldiers fought over the same corner of northeastern France as had their ancestors centuries prior, spilling blood in many of the same fields and experiencing the same fear of death. Indeed, there were many instances of British soldiers fighting in World War I witnessing spectral warriors from the Hundred Years' War rising from the ground to once again do battle with England's enemies. And in the years since World War I, there have been many more sightings of ethereal medieval warriors at Crécy. History is still very close at this battlefield. But just how close?

Foreshadowing Doom at the Firth of Forth

The bridge spanning Scotland's Firth of Forth is a heritage treasure and an engineering masterpiece. Opened on March 4, 1890, at a span of 2587 metres it was, at least until 1917, the longest cantilever bridge in the world, and even today it remains the second longest. It is a major artery connecting the northeast and southeast of Scotland, and at its peak, as many as 200 trains per day rumbled over it. Yet it's only by the good fortune of a prophetic dream that it survived World War I. If not for a moment of paranormal insight by an unassuming retired nurse, it might well have been another casualty of that destructive conflict.

In 1914, Madelaine was an elderly woman, exhausted from decades of nursing in Britain's overcrowded hospitals and enjoying the tranquility of retired life. War had broken out in Europe, but it seemed far away and, if popular assumption was correct, it would surely be over by Christmas. Madelaine refused to let the war intrude upon her idyll that consisted of tending to her flowers, enjoying tea in her garden, and the needlework that kept her mind and fingers agile. We don't always get what we want, however. The war, though distant and of little concern to her, came to Madelaine one night in the midst of a deep sleep.

It was the strangest dream. In it, what looked like grey-colored whales with castles on their backs circled around a pillar rising up from the water. The whales were predatory, and they caused Madelaine to shiver with fear. What's more, they were angular, with sharp, unnatural edges.

And somehow, though she had no idea of the significance at the time, Madelaine instinctively knew these lurking monsters were focusing their vile intent upon "the third pillar," whatever that was. Suddenly, there was a flash of light and the pillar crumbled into the water...

And with a jerk that nearly threw her out of her bed, Madelaine awoke. She took a deep, shuddering breath against the flood of post-dream emotion: a turmoil of fear, confusion and worry. The bedroom was dark and warm and quiet, murmuring with the faint nighttime noises of the town outside the window. She lay back against the pillows, willing herself to calm down and clear her head. Now wide awake, Madelaine stared at the ceiling and wondered what the dream meant.

But it was more than a dream, she instinctively knew. More like a subconscious flash of insight—a piece of a puzzle trying to fit into place. Frowning with concentration into the darkness, the half-remembered dream images started to sharpen. It all meant something; it was a foretelling of a terrible event yet to occur. She was sure of it. But what was she to do with this sudden insight? Who should she tell? Who would believe it was more than just a dream, be able to decipher its meaning, and then get the information to those who could act upon the warning? Madelaine was at a loss.

In the days that followed, she thought long and hard about her dilemma, struggling to decide who to share her dream with. In the end, she decided to tell everyone within her extended social circle, hopeful that someone—anyone—might help. One of her friends, the Countess of Chichester, not only believed that the dream was prophetic but also believed it had specifically targeted the retired nurse. Madelaine's nephew worked for the company responsible for the bridge spanning the Firth of Forth, a bridge supported by pillars rising from the water. The countess urged her friend to write to her nephew immediately and tell him about her dream.

Taking pen to paper, Madelaine related the dream in great detail and then mailed it off. She still had no idea what the vision meant and was uncertain as to whether it was even related the bridge, but she found some consolation in the knowledge that she had done all that was humanly possible.

***

An eerie chill ran through Madelaine's nephew as he read his aunt's letter. He was certain that what she had seen were not whales with castles on their backs, but submarines riding on the surface of the water. And what's more, there was no way anyone, let alone his elderly aunt, could have known that the third pillar in particular on the Firth of Forth Bridge was vulnerable to attack, being the only one not yet reinforced. Should it fall, the bridge would collapse with it. Her dream was a vision of the future, of that he was convinced, and it needed to be acted upon. But how would he go before his superiors? If he approached them and said the warning had come in the form of an old woman's nightmare, they might dismiss it out of hand. He chewed his lip in worry.

In the end, he decided to be completely honest. Standing before the bridge company executives, he swallowed hard and then dove head-first into the incredible story. He stressed that whether one believed in dreams or not, the third pillar was dangerously vulnerable to attack by submarines, which could shell it with their deck guns. And, he added in conclusion, closing the Firth of Forth Bridge, even for a few months, would represent a major strategic victory for the Germans because it would disrupt both economic and military railway traffic. He implored his superiors to correct the oversight and reinforce the pillar.

To his surprise, he was not chased from the room with laughter. The solemn men sitting around the table took his warning seriously and immediately ordered a rearranging of work schedules in order to pack reinforcing concrete around the third pillar of the bridge. And they were just in time.

On September 2, 1914, just one day after work on the supports was completed, German submarine U-21 slipped silently into the Firth of Forth under the cover of darkness. The U-boat's skipper was audacious. He intended to prowl deep into the estuary and then attack the unsuspecting British warships lying at anchor there.

The night was dark, with the moon hidden behind an overcast sky. The submariner, peering through his periscope, looked toward the lights of the dockyard in the near distance. Silhouetted against them, he could make out the dark, brooding outlines of a number of warships. There was a wealth of targets from which to choose: battleships, cruisers and destroyers. U-21 crept slowly along toward its prey, gliding silently just beneath the surface with only a raised periscope to betray its presence. The captain smiled tightly. Leaning comfortably against the bulkhead, he glanced over his instruments and prepared his mind for battle—and victory.

Suddenly, the bright glare of a searchlight flared. It passed across the water once before catching the periscope of U-21 in its beam. Moments later, distant sirens began to echo across the water. The U-boat's skipper was no longer smiling. He cursed violently as his stomach twisted with a sudden, horrible realization. With the alarm raised, U-21 had no chance of a surprise attack on the British ships. Worse, caught in shallow waters of a narrow river, the submarine herself was now vulnerable to attack. In the blink of an eye, fortune had turned against the German aggressor.

Brave but not foolhardy, the U-boat's captain wisely decided to beat a hasty retreat. But not, he grimly thought, before inflicting some damage on the enemy. "Surface the boat!" he commanded. "Gunners topside, clear the deck gun for action. Stand by to fire."

U-21 was now riding on the surface of the Firth of Forth, racing at full speed through the water. As it neared the cantilever bridge, the captain turned his deck gun upon it and rained shell after shell down upon its supporting pillars. The bridge was rocked by multiple explosions. After a few minutes, the captain ordered ceasefire and trained his binoculars upon the bridge. At first, his vision was obscured by a thick cloud of smoke and dust that shrouded the bridge. His heart pounded in his chest. He was anxious to see what devastation the artillery barrage had wrought. Slowly, the cloud cleared, and the skipper cursed. The bombardment had failed to do any significant damage. All the pillars—most recently the third one—had been so reinforced as to be all but immune to enemy shelling. With wounded pride, the captain steered U-21 out of the Firth of Forth and away from the alerted British warships.

Undoubtedly, U-21's captain would have been even more frustrated had he learned that the Firth of Forth Bridge had been saved because of the prophetic dream of an elderly retired nurse who knew nothing about military strategy, enemy vessels or bridge engineering. Madelaine's dream had been a small, but as it turns out significant, contribution to the Allied war effort.

Remembering the Fallen

Bracebridge, Ontario, resident and antique dealer Ted Currie is almost nonplused about the paranormal. "Antique dealers come to expect unusual experiences with heritage items," he says almost casually, reflecting on the widely held belief—and his own personal experience—that spirits can become attached to physical items of personal significance. Nevertheless, while Currie has grown accustomed to spiritual activity over his decades of collecting and peddling antiques, nothing in his past lessened the emotional impact of his ghostly experience on Remembrance Day, 1993.

"It was just weeks before Remembrance Day. I was working, then, from a small basement antique shop, on the upper end of Bracebridge's Manitoba Street," he recalls in his blog. "On this particular overcast Friday afternoon, raining and windy, I was listening to some First World War vintage music I had recorded earlier to play in the shop during the weeks leading up to Remembrance Day.... As we had some Canadian military photos and a minor amount of militaria on consignment from other collectors, the music provided an interesting mood to the lowly lit shop that, by itself, seemed to be a portal back in time."

Indeed, the aged building in which the shop was located had a well-founded reputation for being haunted. Currie knew of this reputation and accepted it as matter-of-fact. When asked what he thought of sharing the building with spectres of the past, he would shrug and offer a smile, saying simply, "I don't mind it at all. Spirits make good company."

Some years before 1993, in his seemingly never-ending quest to uncover new and exciting antiques, Currie happened upon an original and complete World War I uniform that once belonged to a Canadian soldier who, after the war, came to reside in the Bracebridge area. It was a wonderful piece, a rare find, complete with sewn-on insignia, buttons, service medals proudly displayed upon the breast, web gear and helmet. Currie was justifiably proud of the uniform, and he used it frequently for the Remembrance Day displays he arranged every year with whatever artifacts he had available at the time. Displaying the uniform so prominently wasn't a sign of pride in his possession, but rather pride in the men who wore such a uniform in the service of their nation.

"The problem for me was whether to hold on to the uniform, which would likely be the only one I'd ever own in my life, or sell it to a collector as the antique dealer I was supposed to be," Currie says. "There is a fine line between collector and dealer, and sometimes our homes are far more jammed-up with stuff than our actual shops. So I had pretty much decided that following this particular year's Remembrance Day, I would finally attach a price sticker. Reluctantly, but it had to be done. I couldn't collect everything, after all. Suzanne [Ted's wife] still calls me a collector instead of a dealer."

One late October afternoon in 1993, Currie looked up from his desk to see a gentleman he knew standing before him. He was a teacher from one of the local schools, and he seemed fascinated by the uniform that hung just above the counter. One hand fondled it, feeling the rough texture of the material between his fingers.

"Ted," the teacher said tentatively, chewing on his lip in deep thought, his eyes never leaving the uniform, "is there any chance that you would be willing to loan me this uniform for a Remembrance Day play we're putting on next week?"

This soldier, Harry Hind of the 255th Overseas Battalion (Q.O.R.) C.E.F., is just one of so many Canadian men who wore the uniform in the service of their nation during World War I.

As Currie routinely loaned out his antiques as props for community theatre productions, it wasn't a particularly unusual request, and he was happy to do so in this circumstance as well. However, there was one potential problem: the uniform's very modest size. The young Canadian soldier who had worn it into battle had been short and very slight of build. The uniform would fit very few adult males. Currie was about to point out how small it was but suddenly stopped himself from doing so. A quick glance between the teacher and the uniform suggested he was of the perfect size to don it. *What are the odds of that?* Currie found himself wondering.

Currie agreed that it would be great to have the uniform featured in a play commemorating Remembrance Day and all the soldiers who had worn a uniform like this one on behalf of our country. Just to be certain it fit, Currie directed the teacher to an upstairs bathroom and encouraged him to try the uniform on.

"He was gone quite a while, and I wondered if he had just decided to leave after trying it on. That would have been okay, as he thanked me in advance, before he even went upstairs," Currie recalls. "So I just settled down with my writing work again, which at that moment was a wartime story for *The Muskoka Advance*, a Friday paper at that time. The music was sentimental and tear-jerking, and my story was pretty heavy and a little depressing, so when all of a sudden my friend startled me again, I nearly fell off my chair."

"Looks like you saw a ghost, Ted," the man said.

Currie's face had indeed paled. "I did," he stammered as he fought to control his emotions.

"I really can't explain just how ghostly he appeared in that Canadian soldier's uniform," he says today, reflecting back on that startling moment. "It was as if it had been tailored for him. It had an aura that he couldn't have seen, as if the uniform itself was haunted by the past...but somehow, some way accepting of this new body with a strong heart re-animating history.... It seemed as if he had just then walked right out of a military portrait, to stand in front of me for inspection."

Currie admits that he is very seldom at a loss for words, but he was at that moment. He found himself spellbound by the way the uniform fit this man, who had literally just come in off the street, absolutely perfectly.

"He didn't know I had the uniform before he walked into the shop. He was just looking for a military hat or regimental photograph his theatrical group could use as props on stage. Then he found the uniform that no one... not a soul, in two years, had been able to fit into...and yes, many had tried and failed. It was eerie how it all came together that afternoon. It sort of reminded me of Cinderella and the special slipper. They were made for each other," Currie continues.

Just seeing the teacher in that uniform made Currie appreciate the relevance of having kept it those years, long after the time when, as a businessman, he probably should have sold it to make a profit. It was one of those poignant antique dealer moments that he has occasionally experienced, a reminder that his job isn't always about making money but is also about historical preservation. This gentleman, wearing an authentic World War I uniform once owned by a brave Canadian soldier, brought the history Currie adored back to life for a few fleeting but memorable moments down in his dimly lit antique shop.

The teacher looked great on stage, received several compliments from the audience and helped raise lots of money for the Remembrance Day fundraiser. He, and the uniform he wore, helped to remind people of the sacrifices made by our veterans, living and dead, in both World Wars and all other subsequent conflicts.

"Had I seen a ghost? I don't think so," says Currie today. "But as to whether or not I saw the glow of an old spirit when that uniform was full of life again...I think so. I don't see auras, but I do feel them. This one was warm and contented. As an antique dealer, it was just one of those important moments, when you give a little sigh of thankfulness that you've once again had a rare opportunity to experience history all over again...but without bombs going off and machine gun fire over the battlefront trench."

The spirits of the Great War aren't confined to century-old battlefields or melancholy cemeteries where neat rows of crosses mark the resting place of fallen soldiers. Some have returned home, attached to the uniforms or weapons that defined them as soldiers. Undoubtedly, the scars of war have left many of these lingering spirits tormented. But not so in the case of Ted Currie's prized World War I uniform. The energy he felt was positive. Perhaps it was the remains of a soldier proud of his service in the name of king and country but relieved to return to his family at war's end.

If only all the ghosts associated with the First World War could say the same.

Battle for Basra

In 2003, during Operation Iraqi Freedom, the American-led invasion to topple Saddam Hussein from power, British forces were assigned the task of clearing the southern city of Basra. It was to be the second time in a century that the Persian Gulf port would be taken in battle by British soldiers: during the early months of World War I, British and Imperial forces had turned their attention to what was then an Ottoman city.

The Mesopotamia campaign of the First World War put British and Imperial soldiers through all manner of horrors: life-and-death combat, crippling heat, scouring sandstorms, never-ending thirst and the lurking danger of disease. But not all of the horrors they experienced were so easily defined. Some were of the supernatural variety, and were more traumatic simply because soldiers had no way to rationalize what they saw and felt. When British soldiers returned to Basra in 2003, they discovered that the scars of the earlier war had not yet fully healed. The Basra War Cemetery, where fallen Imperial soldiers were buried in 1914, was the subject of frightening tales of ghostly disquiet.

Basra, founded in the year 638, is located on the Euphrates River just inland from where the river flows into the Persian Gulf. In the days of the Abbasid Caliphate, a dynasty that lasted three centuries, it was a vibrant centre for trade and commerce, best known in the West as the home of Sinbad, the heroic, swashbuckling adventurer whose exploits had thrilled listeners for decades. By the time the Ottoman Empire took over the city in 1668, decay had set into Basra, and the city was in the midst of a steep decline from its heyday as a great emporium. Nevertheless, at the dawn of the 20th century, a level of prosperity had returned, centred upon the date trade. In 1912, the export trade totalled 3.2 million pounds, making Basra one of most economically important ports on the Persian Gulf.

Basra was often called the Venice of the East by romanticizing Europeans owing to the city's numerous intersecting canals, but the title was extremely flattering. In truth, Basra was anything but beautiful, consisting of a colourless sprawl of low, flat-roofed homes and businesses that was home to 60,000 people, including a large European merchant class as well as numerous Jews and Armenians. Turks were a minority, consisting mostly of government officials and the local garrison of 4500 men commanded by Subhi Bey.

When relations between the Ottoman Empire and the British Empire became increasingly strained throughout 1914, Britain grew concerned about the safety of British oil supplies in Mesopotamia (as Iraq was then called). Preparations were therefore made to send an expeditionary force from India to capture Basra and secure the Abadan refinery in southern Iraq.

Hostilities between the Ottoman Empire and British Empire formally began on November 5, 1914, and two days later, British Imperial troops secured Abadan, dispersed the light resistance they encountered and established an encampment. Then alarming news reached them: the Turks were encamped in fortified positions and in some strength about six kilometres north at the village of Sahain. Desiring to keep the momentum, the Indian Poona Brigade was told to move out against the enemy.

General W. S. Delamain marched his troops out just after breakfast on November 15, while the rising sun was still just painting the horizon red. The Turkish force was about 2000 men strong, with a few small field guns. They were holding a strong position on the outer edges of a stretch of date plantations that surrounded the village and extended back from the river about three kilometres. Entrenched within the heavy foliage of the date groves, the Turkish strength and disposition was largely masked from the British. Looking through his field glasses, Delamain had only a vague idea of the size of the force opposing him and the layout of their fortifications. Worry clouded his face when he noted his battalions would have to attack across open desert, but the attack must go forward.

As one, the British-Indian troops surged forward at a quick jog, intending to cross the open ground and fall upon the enemy trenches as quickly as possible. The Turks opened fire at 1000 metres with rifles and artillery, though most of the shrapnel exploded harmlessly behind the rapidly advancing ranks. Expecting a stiff fight, the British soldiers were surprised when, after a brief exchange, the Turks fell back in disorder and abandoned Sahain. British casualties in the brief fighting were eight killed and 53 wounded.

November 16 was to be a day of rest for the British, but news came down the river that appeared to make an early movement against Basra imperative. The entire Turkish garrison was advancing south, seemingly intent on a decisive showdown. At the same time, there were rising concerns about the welfare of European citizens who had been detained by Ottoman officials in Basra. The British determined they had to advance immediately, so in the pre-dawn hours of November 17, the entire British force of about 5000 men marched northward.

Contact was established with the Turks at the village of Sahil. The Ottoman forces were arrayed in a strongly entrenched position and had with them 12 field guns. To the British soldiers, it looked like it would be a replay of the fight two days earlier, though the presence of more artillery and a greater number of riflemen promised to make the day bloodier. Worse, the sky suddenly opened up with heavy rain and hail, which quickly turned the ground into a quagmire that would make a rapid advance all but impossible.

The battle began around 10:00 AM when the British ranks began to move forward. The Turks opened a heavy artillery barrage, but again, most shrapnel burst harmlessly overhead. The shin-deep mud made the British advance extremely slow-going; soldiers moved forward at a painful crawl, boots sticking in a morass that exhausted them before they had even reached the enemy trenches. A new wave of heavy and accurate fire crashed into their ranks, but still the attacking infantry advanced steadily and indomitably, apparently unperturbed as companions suddenly cried out in pain and dropped beside them.

When the British were within 400 metres, they bellowed a cry of defiance and levelled their bayonets for a final charge. Turkish morale suddenly broke. The Turks climbed from their trenches and fled. By 4:00 PM, the last of the firing had ceased. Although exact losses for the Turks are unknown, 150 prisoners were taken, their dead numbered in the hundreds, and between 1000 and 2000 men were wounded. There would have been many more casualties had a heat mirage not suddenly hazed the horizon and effectively blinded British gunners firing at the fleeing Turks. Some soldiers took the mirage as supernatural intervention. The day had been costly for the British as well: 38 dead and 315 wounded. But what no one present yet realized was that the grim tally had not only won the field of battle but Basra as well—the Turks abandoned the city to its fate.

When the Imperial troops arrived in Basra on the afternoon of November 21, they found the Arab populace looting the city and black clouds of smoke rising from the Turkish Custom House. Soldiers quickly spread out across the city to impose law and order. For relatively low cost, a historic city and important Persian Gulf port had been won for the British Empire. But in triumph was born hubris that led to four years of terrible fighting in brutal conditions that cost tens of thousands of lives on both sides.

With the battle won and the city captured came the grim task of burying the fallen. British and Indian troops were buried with great care and full honours in a newly established cemetery reserved for Imperial troops killed in Mesopotamia. The Turkish dead were not treated nearly so reverently. Soldiers dug shallow trenches and rolled the bodies in, limbs tangled and one atop another, and then covered them with a thin layer of sand. Such was war a century ago. But in at least one respect it doesn't seem to matter how the deceased were treated: the dead from both burial places—British and Turkish alike—began climbing from their sandy graves to haunt the living.

William Wood was a soldier who took part in the capture of Basra, and he proudly watched as the Union Jack flew over the ancient Mesopotamian city. He didn't believe in ghosts or the supernatural when the war began, but his skepticism was tested one day while leading a patrol near the village of Sahil where the British had defeated the Turks a few months prior.

The patrol began innocently enough. The soldiers were footsore and hot, but there seemed little danger in the palm groves and sand dunes through which they passed. Then with a suddenness that astonished him, a sandstorm rose out of the desert expanse in the distance and raced across the flat terrain to descend upon the patrol. Searing heat and abrasive, sand-laden wind burned the exposed skin on the soldiers' faces and hands. Sergeant Wood adjusted a scarf around his raw cheeks with one hand while the other desperately clung to a tree trunk so the wailing wind wouldn't sweep him away. Unknown to him at the time, the wind also drowned out the terror of one of his fellow soldiers.

When at last the sandstorm died down, the patrol collapsed to the ground in exhaustion, coughing up sand and desperately trying to catch their breaths and recover from the fear caused by the storm. It was only as they were brushing the sand from their clothes, looking around at the altered landscape, that they realized one man in their group was missing. Then they saw prints of long, naked feet leading off into the distance, followed by a trail of blood. Gripping their rifles tightly in their raw hands, the soldiers went off in pursuit of their comrade.

Not 10 minutes later, they came across a mass grave. The sand covering the entwined corpses of fallen Turkish soldiers had been swept away by the raging storm. Wood felt a painful tightening in his gut and knew they were in the presence of evil. The sensation grew stronger as the soldiers followed the footprints and bloody trail into a ruined hovel. Its roof had long since collapsed, and its single room was filled with sand and the debris of a century's abandonment.

The missing soldier was sprawled on the floor, blood staining his uniform red. Squatting over his prone form was the most terrifying thing Wood had ever witnessed, more horrible than anything his worst nightmare could conjure. It looked like it had once been a man, but it was now twisted by evil into a foul mockery of humanity. The figure had a flat nose, a fanged mouth and glowing red eyes. Wild hair whipped around curled horns. It unleashed an inhumanly long tongue, red and swollen, followed by a hollow laugh.

The rest was a blur of rising panic. Wood and his fellow soldiers raised their rifles and fired. The bullets erupted against the wall, passing through the fiend as it dissolved into a smoke-like wisp. As if carried upon a breeze, the dark mist drifted across the room and pressed against the soldiers; it was as cold as ice. Wood said it chilled his veins and numbed every nerve in his body. Worse still was the hot breath that caressed his ear, whispering words that promised his death. Wood felt himself screaming, but he heard no sound. Then, just as he felt he was on the verge of madness, and the numbness in his limbs grew so great he nearly lost the grip on his rifle, the evil vapour swept through the door and out into the desert.

After recovering their senses and their strength, the soldiers recovered their injured comrade—remarkably, still alive—and returned to their unit. But the ordeal was not yet over. Wood endured terrible nightmares every night for weeks afterward, his sleep interrupted by terrible dreams in which whispered words encouraged him to take his own life. He never spoke of it, but he was sure the other members of the patrol endured the same torment. According to Wood, one of the soldiers did indeed shoot himself, while another was hospitalized for mental fatigue—later known as shell-shock and later still as post-traumatic stress disorder.

Was the fiend these soldiers encountered the vengeful spirit of a Turkish soldier? Was it the collective bitterness of those who were callously discarded in a mass grave, their anger given evil form? Or was it some ancient entity from Arabic lore that was drawn to this scene of mass death and suffering? More terrifying to consider is the question of whether this creature continues to haunt the desert around Basra.

The British soldiers who served in Iraq from 2003 to 2013 did not—as far as we know—have to struggle against the torment of this horrifying wraith. But that's not to say they didn't encounter spirits from the First World War. Upon arriving in the country in 2003, British soldiers were saddened to find that the Basra War Cemetery had been neglected during the half-century reign of Saddam Hussein's Baath party. Of the 2551 graves from World War I, hundreds had no headstone owing to vandalism and desecration, while many hundreds more were damaged or decayed. The thought of fallen soldiers lying in foreign soil, their graves abused and their names forgotten, struck a chord with British soldiers. They decided to restore the cemetery as a place of honour.

Soldiers who visited the cemetery averred they could feel the energy of earthbound spirits. There was an uncomfortable heaviness in certain sections, and the presence of undead souls was distinctly felt. More unnerving were the distant voices of the dead carried upon the hot desert wind. One soldier heard a distinct "help me," as a cold-but-unseen hand touched his lower back. In another eerie occurrence, a photo taken inside the cemetery shows a British soldier from behind with what appears to be a smoky, black, disembodied hand near his right shoulder. When the shocked photographer showed the image to the soldier seen in the frame, his comrade was taken aback. He hadn't felt the touch of a hand, but he had experienced an unusually cold caress around the same time. Was this spirit the same one that had whispered a plea for help in the earlier encounter?

Although no one can pinpoint precisely which spirits do not rest in peace in the cemetery, we can assume that trauma over a life cut tragically short or a longing for a distant home might be behind the spirits' restlessness.

With the withdrawal of British and American soldiers in 2013, violence in Iraq has surged. One wonders what this means for the restless Great War dead lying in Iraq's troubled soil. Will the British cemetery once again suffer abandonment and neglect, causing renewed anguish for the soldiers interred there? If it does, it's possible the relatively mild supernatural phenomenon will intensify. And what of the fiend recorded by William Wood? Might the death and suffering of more warfare provide fertile ground for its evil to root? One shudders to think that this horror might still exist, lurking somewhere in the desert, waiting, hungry...

Jersey's Spectral Captives

Ten or so men, legs shackled in irons, shuffled across the sandy field toward a featureless, box-like wooden building in the distance. Although their feet dragged, the men left no trail in their wake, no disturbed sand to mark their passage. Each one wore a grey military uniform, and their hair was cropped short. They looked despondent, forlorn and without hope. A chain securing the building's door suddenly unlocked and fell from the handles. No one had turned a key.

The menacing rattling of the chain stirred the sombre men. Fear crossed their faces. Then the door opened to reveal a dark interior lit only by the single stream of light coming in from the open door. The men blinked hard and rapidly as they marched sullenly into the darkened building and were enveloped by the shadows. When the door slammed shut behind them, they began to cry out in terror. The chain rattled again as it rose up on invisible hands to secure the building once more, trapping the prisoners inside in absolute darkness. The panicked men banged on the door and walls with their fists, but there was no one to hear it. The men were trapped, imprisoned forever on an island far from home…

Mary Bader woke abruptly from her dream, sitting up in bed, her pulse racing. The sheets were tangled around her, and her nightgown was damp with sweat. She sighed, swung her legs over the side of the bed and tried to will her shaking hands to settle down. When at last the tremors subsided, she looked at the nightstand. The light of the clock shone eerily in the dark. It was 3:00 in the morning.

A bad dream, she thought. *That's all it was.*

But—no. Mary couldn't pretend it had been only a nightmare. It had been more than that. It was a memory that she relived while asleep. It had happened. She had seen the events of the dream while on vacation on the Channel island of Jersey. Well, "seen" wasn't quite accurate. "Envisioned" was probably a better way to describe it. She had watched as the misty figures, clearly apparitions, had marched past in irons and disappeared into the blackness of an equally incorporeal building. She had felt their despair.

Driven by the experience and the dream that persistently started to haunt her nights, Mary decided to explore the history of the island. She learned that the sheltered bay in which she had originally had the vision was once the site of a prisoner-of-war camp in which hundreds of German soldiers were imprisoned during the First World War. Mary also learned that the site is rich in paranormal activity. Folklore suggests several German soldiers remain captive there to this day, their restless spirits unable to comprehend that the fences and guards are long gone.

Following the outbreak of war, British authorities found themselves struggling to accommodate the large numbers of enemy prisoners that were falling into their hands. No previous thought had been put toward this matter, so when the number of captured soldiers ran from the hundreds into the thousands, the War Office found itself without the means of dealing with them. There simply weren't enough prison facilities to hold the prisoners, so when the first captured Germans arrived in Britain, they were dealt with in an improvised manner. Nine prison ships were moored in the Thames estuary at Southampton and off Ryde on the Isle of Wight, their cavernous holds transformed into dungeon-like cells.

It was soon clear that permanent prisoner-of-war camps would be needed, but Britain was struggling just to accommodate the soldiers of its own rapidly swelling army. There were few resources left over to facilitate the construction of prison camps. Eventually, however, over the course of the war, 25 camps were built—21 in England, two in Scotland, one in Ireland and one in the Channel Islands—to accommodate the tens of thousands of German prisoners (including 32,272 civilians) held throughout the British Isles.One of the first prison camps was built on the small island of Jersey, part of the Channel Islands. In early August 1914, the British War Office instructed the Jersey authorities to prepare facilities to house prisoners of war. Within a month, Royal Engineers had converted the Royal Jersey Agricultural and Horticultural Society's showground at Springfield, St. Hellier, into a temporary camp. A more permanent location had to be found, though, and eventually, a tract of land on the dune-filled confines of St. Ouen's Bay on the island's west coast was selected to house a more suitable camp. Known locally as Les Blanche Banques, or the White Banks, the area had previously been used as a training ground for the Jersey militia.

Construction began early in 1915, and the camp was ready to receive its first batch of prisoners that spring.

When the ship carrying the first several hundred German prisoners arrived on March 20, a large crowd of curious islanders gathered to catch a glimpse of the "beastly Huns." To the surprise and disappointment of many onlookers that day, the enemy marching off the ship and down the pier turned out to be men just like themselves, many of them no more than boys—a far cry from the monsters painted by propagandists. It must have been hard to relate these young, scared, shell-shocked men to the conquering German hordes that had swept forward in the opening weeks of the war to capture Belgium and push on to the gates of Paris.

At the point of fixed bayonets, the prisoners were marched through the tranquil countryside of the island's far shore and into years of captivity. The camp that awaited them consisted of 40 wooden barrack huts to house the inmates, each one measuring 18 metres long by 4.5 metres wide and capable of holding 30 men. Foundations of low brick or concrete pillars raised the huts off the ground. As well as offering protection from the rising damp, raising the buildings was an expedient way of limiting opportunities for the prisoners to dig escape tunnels in the soft sand. Any attempt to do so would easily be spotted by guards. The camp was completely self-reliant, and its facilities included a cookhouse, a hospital, offices, a store, clerk and staff quarters, an officer's mess and a guard block. The entire camp was surrounded by a three-metre-high wire enclosure that included eight towers where alert guards watched for signs of misbehaviour or attempted escape.

Life at the prison camp was actually surprisingly comfortable, hardly as miserable as Mary Bader's foreboding vision and dreams would suggest. In 1916, *The Times History of the War* painted a picture of daily existence:

> *Twice a day there is a parade, when an officer carefully counts and examines the prisoners, but apart from this the prisoners have nothing to worry them all day, and inside bounds they are free to go where they like and do what they like. The first parade is at 9:30 AM, an hour fixed to prevent the inconvenience of too early rising and too hurried a breakfast. Many of the prisoners lie abed until 8 o'clock. At night, lights must be out by 10:30, and it is forbidden to burn candles. On the whole the Germans...appear to be satisfied with their food, which is certainly more abundant, of better quality, and better served than in corresponding camps in Germany where British prisoners are interned.*

Despite being a model camp, some of the inmates were still determined to break out and return to their homeland. Several actually succeeded in getting past the barbed wire and guards, but in the end, the escapees had nowhere to go. With no way off Jersey and no place to hide out for long, all escapees were eventually recaptured and returned to the prison camp.

The German prisoners remained incarcerated on Jersey until the end of the war. The last of them were returned home in October 1919. The islanders had no use for the camp in the dunes now that the prisoners had departed, and it was dismantled shortly afterward. Soon, the shifting sand claimed much of what remained, leaving only concrete and brick foundations, low walls and the vague outline of former facilities.

The prison camp was gone, but its story didn't end there—not by a long shot. Despite a promise by the British to return all captives to their homes, a few of the Germans were never repatriated: eight prisoners had died of natural causes at the camp, and it seems that their souls have been unable to let go of the mortal world and instead remain imprisoned on the isle of Jersey.

There have been a number of sightings and strange events right up to present. These trapped souls occasionally appear before startled witnesses, and all manner of perplexing poltergeist phenomena has been reported on the grounds of the former prison to remind us of their presence. The sounds of doors slamming interrupt the serenity of the setting, even though no buildings remain. At night, strange lights flicker among the dunes. Anyone who spends any time amidst the one-time camp is left with no doubt of the presence of spirit activity.

We had the chance to correspond with Mary Bader, who shared with us her fascinating paranormal account. While vacationing on the Channel Islands, Mary and her husband spent several days on Jersey. Avid walkers, the Baders enjoyed strolls along the small island's rural lanes, hiking paths and scenic beaches. One day found them on the White Banks. Seduced by the sandy dunes and crystal blue waters, the couple lingered in the bay. They took their shoes off and left them on the sand alongside Mary's handbag and went to cool their feet in the ocean.

Upon returning to their belongings, Mary found the contents of her bag tossed onto the sand, some items as much as a metre away. She thought perhaps the handbag had simply fallen or blown over in a gust of wind and let it go at that. She repacked the bag, and she and her husband continued to explore the bay. A short while later, Mary found her bag inexplicably feeling heavier on her shoulder. Pulling it open, she found it filled with sand and pebbles. Now thoroughly confused and a little unnerved by the whole experience, she and her husband left the beach in a hurry.

Several days later, their vacation was nearing its end. Mary and her husband were still perplexed by what they had experienced at the White Banks beach. The initial fear had subsided to be replaced by curiosity, so they agreed to return there. Mary regrets that decision. They arrived at the site early in the morning. Dew still clung to leaves, and a light fog on the bay was slowly retreating out to sea. Hand in hand, Mary and her husband walked across the beach toward the location where the bag had been left and its contents spilled out during their previous visit. Suddenly, Mary's head began to swim with nausea, and she began swaying on her feet. She felt her husband holding her arm and heard him calling her name, but his voice seemed distant, detached somehow.

Her husband faded from view. The empty bay was no longer quite so empty. All around her were grey, featureless, rectangular buildings. There were guard towers and wire fencing enclosing the beach. Mary was startled by the sudden appearance of about 10 sullen men, each one dressed in a grey military uniform, who had materialized right before her. It was as if an invisible doorway had opened, and the men had marched through it and onto the beach. They appeared so suddenly and so close by that Mary jumped back to remain clear of them.

Chains dangled from their legs and arms as the men marched across the beach toward a distant building. As if by unseen hands, the building's door swung open to reveal an interior as black as coal. It was like a cavernous void of pure shadow penetrated only by a weak stream of daylight from the open door. Heads downcast, the men filed into the building and were swallowed up by the blackness. When the final man had disappeared inside, the door swung shut with a loud bang.

That bang seemed to startle Mary back to her senses. The prison camp faded from view, to be replaced by the concerned face of her husband. He was gently shaking her shoulders, calling out to her, inquiring what was wrong. Light-headed, she collapsed onto the sand, and it was several minutes before she was able to share with him the vision she had seen. It was several minutes longer before strength returned to her legs, allowing her to climb gingerly to her feet and walk back to the car. Later, Mary's sleep was plagued by terrifying nightmares filled with ghostly soldiers tormented by eternal imprisonment.

Not all of the spectral Germans eternally trapped on Jersey remain bound to the grounds of the vanished prison camp. There is at least one exception: the ghost of Carl Brundig. A sailor aboard the warship SMZ *Mainz*, he was captured when his vessel was sunk at the Battle of

Heligoland Bight in August 1914, and he was pulled from the freezing waters of the North Atlantic. The young sailor was eventually sent to the new prison camp on Jersey, and he has the unfortunate distinction of being the first prisoner to die there. His body was buried in the nearby parish churchyard of St. Peter.

Brundig was the only one of the eight German prisoners who died at the camp to be interred in that cemetery. Upon realizing that the camp actually stood in the parish of St. Brelade rather than St. Peter, the rector of St. Brelade insisted that henceforth, all prisoner burials should take place in his churchyard. Why should St. Peter's profit from burial fees when the prison camp wasn't in that parish? The rector won the argument, and all subsequent burials of deceased prisoners happened in St. Brelade's cemetery. The result is that Brundig is alone—and restless—in death. When the moon hangs above and mist gathers around his headstone, Brundig's apparition is said to rise from the soil and walk aimlessly about the grounds. Sometimes he is seen gazing out toward the horizon, as if pondering whether he will ever again see his homeland. The spectral sailor is reported to have an extremely sad demeanor, melancholy and distant.

The tragedy of these Jersey hauntings is that the souls need not remain trapped on the island. In 1961, the remains of the eight POWs buried on Jersey were disinterred, handed over to the German War Graves Authority and returned to Germany, where they were buried in native soil with full military honours. The dead had finally returned home.

But though the physical remains of the soldiers are in Germany, their tortured spirits inexplicably remain imprisoned on the small island where they died. Their restlessness and mindless clinging to the mortal realm chains them in a hellish dungeon of the afterlife. If these apparitions could only see that the obsession that caused them to rise from their graves—a burning desire to return home—has been satisfied, they would undoubtedly find peace and pass from the land of the living to that of the dead, where they belong. Sadly, it seems the ghosts cannot make this connection and are doomed to linger for eternity behind the invisible barriers of the Jersey prison camp. And on certain nights or grey, cloudy days, the undead prisoners remind the world that they are still there.

Mysteries of the *Lusitania*

When the majestic RMS *Lusitania* sailed out of New York Harbor on May 1, 1915, the war in Europe seemed very far away. Aboard ship, the 1959 passengers and crew settled in to enjoy the vessel's famously luxuriant trappings during the week-long voyage to Liverpool, England. There was little fear of the German Unterseeboots ("undersea boats", better known as U-boats), which were preying upon Allied shipping in the Atlantic. *Lusitania* was a neutral ship, and therefore everyone aboard believed it would not be targeted by the Germans. They were tragically mistaken.

On May 7, RMS *Lusitania*, the sister ship of the famously ill-fated *Titanic*, joined her sibling at the bottom of the ocean. When she sank, 1198 innocent souls went down with her. It was a tragedy, every bit as shocking and traumatic as the *Titanic* disaster three years prior. The loss sent both the United States and Great Britain into deep mourning and aroused such anger in America that it helped propel that nation into the war against Germany, turning the tide in favour of the Allied powers and changing the course of history.

The sinking of the *Lusitania* is a disaster cloaked in controversy and shrouded by mystery to this day. Hit by a single German torpedo, the ship was rocked by not one but two explosions. How was that possible? Some theorists suggest *Lusitania* was secretly carrying munitions to Britain and that it was these munitions, touched off by the exploding torpedo, that accounted for the second and fatal eruption. On an even more sinister and callous note, others believe that the First Lord of the Admiralty, Winston Churchill, conspired to allow the *Lusitania* to be sunk in order to bring the rage-fuelled United States into the war. In some eyes, there's compelling evidence to suggest he did just that. And finally, what do we make of the rumours that the ocean liner was secretly carrying more than $20 million in gold bullion at the time of her sinking, a vast treasure that appeared on no ship's manifest? It's a vast tangle of secrets and lies that proves difficult to unravel. We'll look at each of these mysteries in turn.

The most widespread conspiracy involving RMS *Lusitania* suggests the ship was carrying a vast cargo of weapons and ammunition in contravention of military law, and further, that the liner may have been outfitted with guns of its own to serve as an armed auxiliary cruiser. If either rumour were true, the Germans would have been in their rights to attack and sink the vessel.

The *Lusitania*, sunk by a German torpedo in 1915, is even today the subject of controversy and conspiracy theories.

On the afternoon of May 7, the German submarine U-20 fired a single torpedo at the *Lusitania*. It ran straight and true, smashing into the hull, exploding and tearing a gash in her side. At first, the wound didn't appear fatal. The ship's captain was convinced his ship could stay afloat and therefore didn't immediately order lifeboats lowered. A short while later, however, there was a second, even larger explosion that literally ripped the vessel wide open. She sank so rapidly and at such a steep angle (her bow was already on the seabed when her stern lifted clear of the water) that it was difficult to get more than a handful of lifeboats away, which explains the unusually high death toll of nearly 1200 souls.

If U-20 didn't fire a second torpedo—and her logs insist that she did not—then what caused the second explosion that ultimately sealed the doom of the ship and so many of her passengers? One long-held theory has it that the second explosion came from the detonation of a cargo of contraband munitions hidden in the liner's holds.

Under the terms of the Hague Convention governing the rules of war, a submarine had to stop and search a passenger liner for contraband before it could sink her, and additionally had to allow a reasonable time for passengers to safely abandon ship. However, there was one exception: if the ship in question had been armed as an auxiliary cruiser, it was deemed a military vessel and could be sunk without any warning whatsoever. Germany always claimed that the *Lusitania* was an armed merchant cruiser carrying troops from Canada, but Britain insisted she carried no troops, had no guns, and that her only cargo was 5000 cases of harmless bullet and shell fuses. Who is right?

During the exhaustive post-incident hearings, not a single passenger claimed to have seen guns on the ship's decks, and official cargo manifests support the British assertions as to the nature of the ship's cargo. But what if the guns were disguised and the manifests were falsified? Some researchers have asserted that in addition to the acknowledged cargo, the *Lusitania* carried a secret cargo that included 46 tons of aluminum powder, which was used in the manufacture of explosives, as well as a large quantity of nitrocellulose (gun cotton). Either of these materials could have been set off by the torpedo explosion and been responsible for the second, fatal eruption.

The story doesn't end with wartime accusations, however. During the 1950s, the Royal Navy apparently dropped dozens of depth charges over the wreck during what were labelled anti-submarine exercises. Were the exercises used to mask what were attempts to mangle the wreck so badly as to destroy any evidence of deck guns and secret cargo?

Noted maritime historian Professor William Kingston of Trinity College, Dublin, believes the British are involved in an elaborate cover-up and that Germany was fully justified in sinking the *Lusitania*, saying, "There's no doubt at all about it that the Royal Navy and the British government have taken very considerable steps over the years to try to prevent whatever can be found out about the *Lusitania*." Is there a chance that the truth may still lie at the bottom of the Irish Sea?

Allegations of a darker conspiracy involving the *Lusitania* centre upon the claim that Winston Churchill, in his role as First Lord of the Admiralty, colluded with Admiral Jack Fisher and other senior Royal Navy officers to place the helpless ocean liner in danger of prowling U-boats, anticipating that if the ship went down with heavy loss of American lives, it would hasten the entry of the United States into the war. The origins of this conspiracy are traced to a conference hosted by the Admiralty on May 5, 1915, just two days before the *Lusitania* was sunk. It was there that a decision was supposedly made to withdraw the *Lusitania*'s naval escort without notifying her captain, leaving the ship alone and vulnerable in waters where U-boats were known to be active.

Perhaps the most damning evidence of a government conspiracy is the presence at this meeting of a relatively obscure naval intelligence officer, Lieutenant Commander Joseph M. Kenworthy, the lone junior officer in a roomful of admirals. What was such a low-ranking officer doing at a meeting attended by the most powerful men in the Royal Navy? It seems that Kenworthy's only relevance was having previously submitted a report, commissioned by Churchill himself, assessing the political impact should a passenger liner carrying a large number of Americans be sunk by the German navy.

Conspiracy theorists are certain that Churchill and the Royal Navy planned to manipulate events so that this very scenario played out. The *Lusitania* and her passengers would be sacrificed in an effort to lure the United States into the war against Germany. Adding to the evidence against Churchill was a letter he wrote to Walter Runciman, President of the Board of Trade, just one week before the tragic sinking of the *Lusitania*, in which he coldly suggested that it was "most important to attract neutral shipping to our shores, in the hope especially of embroiling the United States with Germany."

There are some holes in the theory that Churchill and other senior members of the Royal Navy conspired to put the liner in harm's way, however. Records from the May 5 conference clearly indicate that Royal Navy ships stationed in Ireland were in fact instructed to escort the *Lusitania*, not leave her to her own devices. It's also a matter of record that at least eight warnings of U-boat activity off the coast of southern Ireland were passed along to the *Lusitania* by the Royal Navy on May 6 and 7. Furthermore, as a protective measure against enemy submarines, the Navy directed the liner's skipper to steer a zig-zag course and to stay clear of land because ships were easier to see from periscopes when silhouetted against a solid background—these sound instructions were inexplicably ignored. Passing along warnings and suggesting precautions hardly seems the behaviour of an institution bent on setting the *Lusitania* up for disaster.

Still, there is the matter of the naval escorts that failed to materialize, the refusal of the *Lusitania*'s captain to answer several questions in the post-sinking inquiry on the grounds of wartime secrecy imperatives, and the fact that the British government continues to this day to keep secret certain documents relating to the final days of the voyage; even the records that are available are often missing critical pages. You be the judge if the *Lusitania* was the target of a cold-hearted conspiracy or simply one more victim of a vicious war.

There is one last mystery surrounding the *Lusitania*, one that has tantalized treasure hunters ever since the ship sank. It has been reported that when she sank, the ship was carrying in her holds $20–25 million in gold bullion. Never listed on any official document, no one knows where this gold originated, why it was kept secret or what its ultimate purpose was. Was it a secret payment from the government of the still-neutral United States, or from wealthy private citizens of that country, to help pay Britain's war debts and keep her fighting? Some versions of the story state that Royal Navy divers recovered the gold from the wreck sometime in the 1940s or '50s; others suggest the gold may still lie in the twisted hulk at the bottom of the ocean. Of course, we don't know for certain if a cargo of gold was ever even on the ship, and perhaps we'll never know.

There are a pair of paranormal footnotes to this whole drama of confounding mysteries and byzantine plots, both of which are as incredible as the loss of life aboard *Lusitania* was tragic.

Just as the mighty liner was slipping beneath the waves, the *Lusitania*'s commanding officer, Captain William Turner, jumped over the side and into the icy water. He thrashed his arms and kicked his legs, trying to get back to the surface. It took him a moment to realize that he didn't know which way was up. Everything was black. His lungs were desperate for air. Turner thrust forward, trusting that he was swimming toward the surface.

Suddenly his face was in the air again and he gasped. He watched in silent horror as his ship disappeared from view. There were no lifeboats in sight. Spitting out sea water, he looked in the direction of the Irish coast several kilometres away. Turner was a strong-willed man, and rather than give in and allow himself to slip beneath the waves for good, he decided to swim for shore. If he was going to be claimed by the ocean, it would be only after he had put up a desperate fight. Hours later, exhausted and chilled to the bone, Turner crawled ashore on a rocky beach off Old Head of Kinsale, Ireland, and lay there shivering. There would be no watery grave for him—one less name added to the grim roll call of those who had gone down with the *Lusitania*.

Turner's epic swim was incredible enough, but as the story of his survival circulated in the media over the next few days, an unbelievable wrinkle emerged. Exactly 50 years earlier from the day the *Lusitania* went down, on the first day of his maiden sea voyage, then–cabin boy Turner found his ship sinking beneath him at nearly the exact same spot where the *Lusitania* went down. As the stricken ship rolled onto its side and sank to the bottom, young Turner dove overboard but couldn't find a lifeboat. Desperate, he began to swim toward the coast of Ireland. Hours later, shaking uncontrollably with cold and exhaustion, he stumbled from the surf at Old Head. It was precisely the same swim, exactly half a century apart. What were the odds of that, an incredulous press asked. Pure coincidence or something else we can't explain—fate, divine intervention, some paranormal force—at work.

Captain Turner was understandably deeply scarred by the tragedy of the *Lusitania*'s sinking and felt personally responsible for the heavy loss of life. As skipper of the ship, the welfare of all those aboard was his responsibility, and he took that pledge very seriously. Captain Turner felt that the blood of the 1198 people who died was on his hands. Would they have been saved had he followed the recommended zig-zag course once he neared his destination?

The events of the aftermath certainly didn't help absolve him of the guilt he burdened himself with. Even though he was an experienced sailor and one of the Cunard line's more respected commanders, the British government tried to pin official blame for the sinking squarely on his shoulders. It was a heavy blow for Turner, like a punch square in the gut that leaves you gasping for air. Even when the inquiry cleared his name, reasoning that many ships were sent to the bottom even while performing evasive manoeuvres, the lifelong mariner still felt wounded by the public questioning of his competence and responsibility.

Cleared of all charges, Captain Turner was given a new command: the SS *Ivernia*, another Cunard liner that in peacetime had run between Italy and New York. Since the war had erupted, the vast ship had been in the employ of the British government, serving as a troopship transporting soldiers to distant battlefields. History repeated itself for Captain Turner when, at 10:12 AM on January 1, 1917, the *Ivernia* was torpedoed by the submarine UB-47 about 100 kilometres southeast of Cape Matapan, Greece. Thanks to rapid orders to make for lifeboats and to rescue vessels racing to the scene, only 120 men lost their lives, but coming so quickly on the heels of the *Lusitania* disaster, it shook Captain Turner to the core. He became despondent, moody and on the verge of emotional collapse. Turner was awarded the Order of the British Empire (OBE) for his service to the Crown during the war, but he was haunted by both the loss of life and self-doubt, and he retired less than a year later.

During both wartime sinkings, Captain Turner had with him the same pocket watch. It was a treasured item that he carried for the rest of his life. Recently, this watch was donated to the Merseyside Maritime Museum in Britain, and it's reputed that the museum got more than it bargained for. The donation may have included the restless spirit of the mariner, still haunted by the loss of *Lusitania* and *Ivernia*, bound forever to his watch.

Just try to imagine for a moment how traumatic it would be to survive the sinking of two ships for whose well-being you were responsible while more than 1300 passengers drowned. The guilt would become almost unbearable, your own personal hell. It's that oppressive feeling of sheer hopelessness that some people claim to feel when in close proximity to Turner's pocket watch.

It's doubtful that Turner could have done anything to save either ship once it was spotted by a lurking U-boat, but his guilt caused his spirit to refuse to pass on to the next level of existence. His soul is trapped between two worlds, bound to his watch; the Merseyside Mariner Museum is his prison. A shadowy outline of a person was once caught in a picture of the exhibit containing the watch. Two separate mediums who visited the museum saw the image of a lone man in uniform, an elderly gentleman with snow white hair and sad features, standing near the watch. They instinctively knew this forlorn figure was the watch's owner. Another individual admiring the watch heard a voice as dry as sandpaper calling out his name. He turned to see who was hailing him, but found no one. He was completely alone in the gallery.

The oceans of the world jealously guard their secrets within their cold, dark depths. As a result, the truth behind the tragic loss of the *Lusitania* may well remain a mystery forever. She lies at the bottom of the Atlantic Ocean, her hull the eternal grave of more than a thousand souls. Perhaps the spirits of the dead prefer it this way. As long as the mysteries remain, *Lusitania* and those who perished aboard her will be remembered.

Ghouls of No Man's Land

Although no soldier looked forward to battle, the terror of facing the fire of machine guns and the explosive fury of artillery was nothing compared to what horrors hid within the desolated expanse of the No Man's Land between the two opposing sides. Stories of lone sentries going missing during the night, of patrols stumbling upon corpses that looked as if they had been chewed upon by human teeth, of mysterious figures seen clawing forth from the earth at the bottom of a shell hole and then shuffling away in the gloom…all were unnervingly common and horrified even the most hardened soldier. In some cases, these legends and tales were simply the byproduct of the suggestive power of the grim and desolate battlefield's hideous mystique, but many men believed some of the stories were very much true: that not all the dead remained dead, and that they fed—and perhaps still feed—ravenously on a grisly meal of their fellow man.

Creatures of gut-churning horror, these ghouls were the result of some blasphemous curse that compelled them to rise from where they fell in battle to prey upon the living. Crazed by ravenous hunger for human flesh, they silently stalked the desolate wastes of No Man's Land, gorging on rotten corpses or on flesh stripped fresh from the newly dead or even from still-living bone. They were doomed never to find peace from either their tireless appetite or the torment of their undead existence. Most of the time, one only knew a ghoul was in the vicinity when a buddy went missing and all that could be found were fragments of shredded uniform and a few gnawed bones at the bottom of a shell hole.

Ghouls were a byproduct of the nature of warfare on the Western Front. On France's World War I battlefields, one entered a land of the dead. It was a hellish realm that you or I today, in the comfort of our homes, can hardly even imagine—an earth-eviscerated desolation that stretched the breadth of France from the English Channel to the borders of Switzerland. Thousands of corpses in varying degrees of decomposition littered the landscape, and the odour of rotting flesh wafted out to the living in waves of gut-churning stink. The stench was so foul it worked its way into clothing and into food. Men sometimes went hungry rather than eat, having no appetite for the spoiled rations.

Living conditions were nightmarish. Soldiers existed in a near-subterranean world, eating and sleeping in deep trenches and underground warrens, sharing their space with rats and other vermin. It wasn't lost on the soldiers that the trenches they dug and in which they lived looked remarkably like extended graves. Sometimes, that's just what they were. A massive artillery bombardment might collapse an entire stretch of trench line, burying dozens of men alive in one stroke. Other times, a partial trench collapse might be less deadly but no less horrifying if the collapsed wall revealed mouldering bodies long buried. There are numerous stories of soldiers living for days or weeks on end with skeletons of fallen enemies or comrades protruding from the walls, desensitized to the horror by constant exposure to death.

The horrors of trench warfare included living side by side with the dead—and possibly undead.

Vermin and rotting corpses…these were far from the most terrifying things awaiting the soldiers on the front lines. Sentries on duty at night peered anxiously into the dark, fearful of what might be looking back at them, hungry, evil and undead. One of the many trench rumours passed from unit to unit focused on a band of deserters that lived in the wilds of No Man's Land, reduced to stripping the dead of food and belongings and even, some whispered, eating the flesh of the fallen. There was a widespread belief that these fiendish stalkers were in fact dead themselves, soldiers who had clawed forth from shallow graves to haunt and hunt the living. Two particular fears lie at the heart of these stories: the fear of dying and the fear of cannibalism.

Imagine for a moment the fear of a young soldier, still a teenager as many were, as he prepared to go out on a nighttime patrol of the desolate land between the opposing armies. As he cleaned and loaded his rifle, secured his gear so it wouldn't rattle and give away his location to the enemy, and perhaps tried to swallow a hasty meal in a mouth bone-dry with fear, his mind would have been preoccupied with the terror of what lay ahead in the gathering darkness. From the moment he and his fellow soldiers climbed over the top of the trench to begin their patrol, all that lay ahead was danger and possibly death. His palms would have sweated at the thought of being killed in an enemy ambush or being obliterated by an artillery round that landed in their midst. If he lost his way in the dark, he could end up in enemy lines and captivity. And, most terrifying of all, he had heard the older soldiers whispering of the monsters lurking in the darkness. These men, veteran soldiers the youngster would have looked up to, who had bravely fought in battle, were terrified of being captured and murdered by cannibalistic ghouls said to lurk in the dark. The fear of the unknowns hiding in the blackness would have played on any man's mind.

Sometimes, however, fear of the unknown became terror in the face of horrifying realities.

The blackness of night had descended on the war-torn landscape, and with it, fog had rolled in like a misty grey blanket. Huddled together at the bottom of a shell hole, mud-caked blankets pulled tight to their chins in an effort to ward off the evening chill, two soldiers sought rest after an exhausting day. Although bone-weary, sleep evaded them.

The moon was high in the sky, dimly visible through the veil of fog, when both men heard the sound of nearby movement. Tossing aside his blanket, one of the soldiers—a grizzled sergeant—sat up and peered over the rim of the shell hole, his eyes trying to penetrate the blackness. His companion, awake as well, joined him at the lip and followed his gaze.

"I don't see anything," the younger soldier said in a hushed whisper, tension clear in his voice. He had been in France for only a few weeks, and fear lined his freckled face.

The sergeant dropped back into the hole where the two of them had bedded down for the night. "Neither do I. Now. I saw something, though. It was just a shadow, but there was something there. It could be one of our men, maybe someone lost or wounded."

"Or it could be a trap," the young private said. He swallowed loudly, his eyes wide in the dark.

"There's one way to find out," the sergeant smiled. He reached for his rifle and then drew his trench knife. The straight steel blade made a faint hissing sound as it cleared the scabbard. "You stay here," he commanded as he crawled from the hole.

The night was as silent as it was dark. The sergeant's pulse beat in his neck as he inched forward through the mud. He moved stealthily, his senses alert to any sign of danger. He had advanced perhaps 30 metres into the devastated wasteland when he caught a whiff of decay hanging

in the chill night air. His eyes strained. Was there someone up ahead, a shadow moving in the darkness, shuffling
through the gloom?

There was little time to consider it. The hiss of an artillery shell in flight alerted the sergeant to a more immediate danger. With only seconds to react, he jumped to his
feet and raced for the cover of the closest shell hole.
He never made it. There was a sensation of heat and deafening noise, and his breath was punched from his chest.
The soldier was thrown off his feet by the force of the
explosion, landing on his back in an eruption of pain.
Warm blood from a scalp wound flowed freely down his
face, pooling in his eyes and blinding him. With shaking
hands he tried to wipe the blood away, but it was no
use—it kept coming in an endless stream of crimson.

The sergeant lay there in pain and misery for a few
moments. Perhaps it was longer. He may have passed out.
But he was suddenly snapped back to his senses by the
realization that something felt wrong. The pall of death
suffused the area like a wet blanket; an unearthly chill
iced his blood. Footsteps, half dragging through the
slurping mud, approached slowly. A tremor of terror ran
through him.

The sergeant could sense it was looming over him. Still
blinded, he couldn't see who or what it was, but he could
feel its presence, and a fresh wave of chills ran down his
spine and goose-pimpled his flesh. Something seemed to
reach down into his chest, slowly squeezing the air from
his lungs, and he found himself gasping for breath.

"Who are you?" he asked in a voice hoarse with fear
and pain.

There was no reply. He could sense its silent mockery, though. With an arm that ached with pain, he reached for the bayonet at his belt, but a booted foot pressed down on his wrist, pinning his arm in place.

"Who the hell are you?" he demanded now, growing fear and anger making his voice raspy.

The presence chuckled—a liquid, putrescent sound, accompanied by a wave of graveyard stink. The soldier fought down panic. He felt certain he was going to die this night.

Bony fingers reached down to wrap around his throat, carrying the same sapping chill as a cold winter's night. He tried to fight back, but his arms and legs felt weary and heavy, numbness spreading through his body. As his attacker leaned in, he caught another whiff of the grave. He gagged at the clammy touch and gut-churning reek, and as the bony fingers tightened around his neck, he felt his life slipping away. It seemed easier to give in to death than to fight any longer.

Distantly, the sergeant registered the sound of another nearby explosion and felt another wave of heat and concussive blast roll over him. Suddenly, the fingers choking his life away were gone, the presence looming over him no more. It simply disappeared, gone in the span of a heartbeat.

The sergeant didn't know how long he lay there, shivering and sweating, scared that his assailant might return at any moment to finish the job. But it didn't. When his fear had subsided and some of his strength returned, the sergeant rolled onto his stomach and began crawling through the mud, blindly navigating the wreckage of the landscape, hoping he was headed toward friendly lines. As luck would have it he was, and it wasn't long before he was recuperating in an aid station. His injuries were relatively superficial, but no bandage could cover the horror of that night's experience; no medication could dull the memories of it that flooded back whenever he slept; and no sutures could close the terrible unseen wounds.

Some readers might dismiss these ghouls as nothing more than fantasy, but no one could tell this soldier—a courageous veteran of several battles, who had killed and in turn watched his friends be killed, and who had stoically endured privations and suffering the likes of which we can hardly imagine—that grisly monsters of some sort weren't hunting men under the cover of darkness. He had encountered one, and by some strange twist of fate had lived to tell of it.

Death seemed to stalk every man on the Western Front, and men began to honestly believe death was literally a lifeless corpse that waited for victims. Maybe they weren't wrong.

Cursed U-Boat

Sometimes, when a terrible storm kicks up in the seas surrounding the British Isles, the raging winds carry the moans of inhuman cries. Out of the stormy spray, the rusted hulk of a spectral U-boat rises from the depths, glowing eerily against the blackness of the night sky, manoeuvring with a supernatural grace unaffected by the squall. Faded white letters on the misty conning tower read "UB-65."

At the bottom of the ocean lie the physical remains of UB-65, the underwater tomb of her crew of 34 men. Partially ripped asunder by the explosion that sent her to her doom, the submarine rests tilted at an awkward angle on the seabed. If you were to swim through the tear in the boat's hull, daring the sightless depths within, you would find a morbid scene of skeletons lying against the bulkheads, twisted in tormented positions by the agony of their final, drowning moments. UB-65 is a true ghost ship. Interestingly, the hauntings actually began before she and her crew went to their watery grave.

By the spring of 1916, after almost two years of fighting, the battlefields of Belgium and France were literally awash with blood. Hundreds of thousands of men had died, and the two sides were still locked in a stalemate. Only at sea did there appear to be the opportunity for a decisive breakthrough. Germany's U-boats (submarines) were taking a heavy toll on British shipping, with hundreds of ships carrying vital supplies having been sent to the bottom of the Atlantic. Germany was convinced that its navy, not its army, would lead the way to victory and began devoting much of its war effort toward producing more and more submarines to starve Britain into submission.

One of the new subs being built in 1916 was UB-65. In most respects, she was little different than any of hundreds of other U-boats in the German navy. But there was one key difference: from her very beginning, UB-65 was cursed, infused with a festering evil that plagued her crew throughout her unlucky existence.

UB-65 was laid down at the Vulcan Werke shipyard, in Hamburg, and almost immediately gained an evil reputation. Only seven days after construction began, a steel girder broke free of the chains suspending it overhead and crashed down onto the newly laid hull. A worker was crushed beneath its massive weight and lay there, in agony, for almost an hour while frantic efforts were made to rescue him. Finally the girder was lifted away, but by then it was too late. The man had died just moments before. A subsequent inquiry looking into the accident could find no fault in either the chains suspending the girder or the methods of the work crew. There was nothing to explain how the girder broke free. It was a mystery.

Workers knew different. They knew there was a reason for the accident. Simply stated, UB-65 was cursed, and all those who worked on her or served on her did so at their own peril. She became known as an iron coffin, a ship of evil reputation that took innocent lives. Although it sounds like superstition run wild, this label proved well justified as a string of mysterious, tragic incidents unfolded aboard her.

It seemed everything that could go wrong during construction, did. The most alarming tragedy occurred just before the U-boat was completed when, during a routine test, the engine room compartment rapidly filled with deadly chloride gas. Three engineers were overcome by the choking fumes, collapsing before they could escape to fresh air. All three men died.

UB-65 was finally launched on June 26, 1917, and there was no one at the shipyard sorry to see her sail away. Sadly for her new crew, there was to be no reversal of fortunes for the cursed submarine merely because she had left the shipyard. Whatever evil influence dogged the boat during construction followed her out of port and would continue to bedevil her throughout her career.

On her shakedown trials in the North Sea, a crew-member was mysteriously lost overboard. The official report was that the sailor was washed overboard during a fierce storm. The story whispered by sailors was more ominous. It was said that the young mariner simply climbed down from the conning tower and walked, without looking left or right, straight off the deck and into the cold sea. Something had possessed him and compelled him to take his own life. In either event, the body was never recovered.

Later, during the same shakedown cruise, the captain decided to dive the boat beneath the waves to test the seaworthiness of her hull. She dove 10 metres deep, then 20, then 30. Suddenly, an alarm sounded from the engine room. A ballast tank had sprung a leak, allowing sea water to pour into the submarine. The batteries that powered the boat while submerged were damaged by the flooding, and consequently, UB-65 was dead in the water. She sank like a stone, settling on the seabed as the nervous crew listened to her hull pop and groan under the depth pressure.

Hour after hour she rested on the ocean floor while the crew struggled to find a way to float her upward. As she lay immobile, the same deadly chloride gas fumes from the electric batteries that had already claimed three lives began to fill the engine room. The crew worked feverishly to repair the damage and get the ship to the surface, knowing that eventually they would all either perish from the deadly fumes or suffocate from lack of oxygen. After 12 nerve-wracking hours, the U-boat finally began to rise to the surface. When at last it breached the waves, all of the crew raced on deck and into the blessed fresh air. Amazingly, everyone survived, and the cursed submarine managed to limp back to Germany for repairs. No rational explanation for the incident was ever found.

UB-65's run of misfortune continued unabated. After several days of hurried repairs, the submarine was again readied for sea and what would be her first combat cruise. But as torpedoes were being loaded aboard, the U-boat was rocked by a deafening explosion. One of the torpedoes had mysteriously exploded, instantly killing the executive officer and five crewmen. The ship's death toll had jumped to 11 men, and she had yet to even see combat.

As the dead were being buried with full naval honours at Wilhelmshaven and another round of repairs was made, another inquiry was held, looking into the misfortune aboard UB-65. Was there an engineering fault?

Perhaps a problem with procedures? Maybe crew training or the orders of the commanding officers were at fault? After weeks of investigation, the inquiry could come up with nothing that would reasonably explain the explosion. It was yet another mystery.

Weeks later, the repaired UB-65 was finally ready to be put to sea. But just hours before the submarine was to throw off its mooring lines, a young, ashen-faced sailor raced up to the skipper. His eyes were wide with terror, his lips quivered, and he shook uncontrollably. When at last he had calmed down enough to speak, the sailor swore to have seen the deceased executive officer aboard. The captain naturally dismissed such talk as nonsense. He scolded the young man for drinking too much on leave and for letting nerves over the submarine's first combat patrol to get the better of him. The Imperial German Navy expected more from its men, the captain lectured. The rebuke did little to assuage the fears of the young sailor. Unable to bring himself to sail aboard a haunted submarine, he deserted the vessel.

It wasn't long before another member of the crew claimed to have seen the ghost of the dead officer aboard ship. Faced with this second report of a ghost sighting, even the stoic captain had reason to pause. The sailor explained how he had watched the apparition stroll up the gangplank, then walk toward the bow and stare out at the sea before vanishing into thin air.

It was now difficult for the captain to dismiss the story completely, but what was he to do? And why was his former executive officer, a man he had called a friend, spiritually damned in death? These were questions he didn't have ready answers for. But one thing the captain knew for certain: whether or not there was indeed a ghost aboard, the navy expected UB-65 to do her duty at a critical time in the war. And so, whatever reservations he may have had, he ordered the U-boat put to sea.

The submarine actually enjoyed some early success, sinking an Allied merchant ship only days into her inaugural patrol. In the excitement, talk of the ghost began to wane. Then a second ship was sent to the bottom. As most of the men aboard UB-65 erupted in applause and cheers, the mood in the engine room was far different. There, it was deathly silence. Several sailors, all the colour drained from their faces, stood rooted with fear, watching as the dead-and-buried first officer carefully studied instrument panels, going about his duties as if he remained a part of the flesh-and-blood crew. More than a dozen men saw the ghost that day.

Word of the sighting spread quickly through the vessel, and soon the captain had a crisis on his hands. The crew was terrified and on the verge of mutiny, demanding they return to Germany and be posted to other submarines. Morale, critical to operating in the close confines of a U-boat, plummeted to such a degree that the captain was fearful they would refuse to carry out his orders. He did his best to dispel the nervous talk and retain the crew's loyalty, but it was a losing battle. During the remainder of UB-65's cruise, the sullen crew sank only one more British ship. They were more concerned with surviving the patrol than with fighting the war.

When the boat returned to base, the sailors shared their terrifying experiences with fellow sailors, and soon rumours of the ghostly stowaway aboard UB-65 spread throughout the entire armada. Men began refusing to sail aboard her—the very last thing Germany needed at this desperate time in the war. It was only through threats of harsh discipline that sailors could be compelled to report for duty.

By January 1918, even the captain could no longer dismiss the sightings of an apparition aboard ship as the rantings of foolhardy, superstitious or over-imaginative seamen. Finally he too had seen the ghost of his former first officer. The startling sighting came as the U-boat was prowling the English Channel, stealthily hunting for enemy ships. A winter storm was pounding the area, making the seas particularly rough. The skipper decided to surface the boat and ride out the worst of the weather. Lashed by driving rain and sleet, with waves pounding over her hull and against the conning tower, UB-65 sailed onward. As was customary whenever a submarine surfaced, lookouts were posted on the tower to keep a vigilant watch for enemy ships or aircraft.

One of the lookouts grew alarmed when he spotted an officer standing on the wave-lashed deck. The sailor couldn't believe any man would be reckless enough to venture out on the deck in this storm. A wave would surely carry him overboard. The sailor desperately called for the officer to return, but his words were drowned out by the fury of the storm. Then, realization dawned on him. There couldn't possibly be anyone on the deck. All hatches were battened down and secured, except the one from which he himself had climbed onto the conning tower, and no one could have gotten by him unnoticed.

The only explanation was that the officer standing before him was the wraith of the dead first officer.

In a voice hoarse with terror, the crewman screamed down into the submarine that the ghost was once again aboard. Hysteria broke out below deck, as by now the sailors were certain the ghost's appearance was a harbinger of doom. The captain, struggling to maintain control, raced up the ladder to see for himself what had gotten the lookout so worked up. He fully expected to see nothing. Imagine his surprise when he, too, saw a man standing on the deck in defiance of the waves crashing over it. Then that same man turned slightly, revealing his face. Colour drained from the skipper's cheeks and a knot formed in stomach. Standing before him was his one-time first officer, who he himself had helped bury months before. Seconds later, the ghost vanished.

When the U-boat returned to port, Kriegsmarine officials ordered her officers and crew rounded up for questioning. They knew that submariners were the bravest of sailors, each one possessing nerves of steel that allowed them to endure long hours of confinement deep below the ocean's surface, to face bombardment by enemy warships dropping deadly depth charges from above, and to put to sea despite the fact that they had only a 50/50 chance of ever returning from a patrol. Navy officials knew that the ghost stories about UB-65 couldn't be dismissed as the irrational ranting of cowards; at the same time, neither could they simply admit the ship was haunted. The damage such an admission would inflict on morale fleet-wide would have been devastating. High-ranking officers questioned the crew of UB-65 in an attempt to find a rational explanation, but in the end they were unable to find anything that might explain the rash of ghost sightings. Finally, in exasperation, they decided it was simply easier to break up the crew and send them off to other assignments.

But that wasn't the end of the UB-65's career. In its life and death struggle, Germany needed every vessel it had. The German navy sought help from a Belgian pastor of the Lutheran church to exorcise the ghost of the restless officer, hoping that whatever taint cursed the submarine would be wiped clean by prayer. The exorcism was carried out at Bruges with several anxious high-ranking German officers looking on with a mixture of fascination and dread. When the rite was complete, everyone breathed a sigh of relief, certain that the submarine had been cleansed and could be put back into service.

A new crew was assigned to the purified UB-65. For a while, it did indeed seem as if the undead officer had finally passed over to the other side. For several months, there were no sightings of the forlorn apparition, and the captain, a stern disciplinarian, let it be known that he would not tolerate any talk of ghosts and hauntings and curses aboard his ship.

Then, as if to spite the captain, in May 1918, the ghost materialized once again. During a patrol in the Bay of Biscay, the dead officer was seen at least three times by three separate individuals. One of these bewildered men was a petty officer who swore that he saw the ghost slip through a solid iron bulkhead and pass into the engine room, while another watched him stand on the deck, his ethereal hair whipping in the wind as he gazed out to the horizon.

A third crewman, a torpedo handler named Eberhardt, claimed the ghost haunted him at night, tormenting his sleep and preventing him from resting. The seaman became so disoriented and confused by terror and lack of sleep that he degenerated into a slavering maniac. Eberhardt had to be put under guard to prevent him hurting others or himself. Sadly, when the submarine surfaced to recharge its batteries, a raving Eberhardt broke free of his guards and committed suicide.

The shocked crew was still mourning his loss the next morning when another seaman, a young man named Meyer, raced up onto the deck, pushed past other crewmen and leaped into the English Channel. He was last seen being carried away on the waves toward a tragic watery death. He had been so desperate to escape the submarine, which by now most aboard considered little more than a steel coffin infused with the very essence of death, that he chose to dive into the vast expanse of water knowing he would never reach shore. Meyer was never seen again.

Not long afterward, the submerged UB-65 was attacked by a destroyer of the British Royal Navy and forced to hide on the seabed. As she sat silent and unmoving on the ocean floor, with thunderous explosions ripping apart the ocean all around her, the terror that had taken hold of the crew reached new heights when the interior of the boat began to glow with a greenish light. There was no source for the illumination, no possible explanation. Finally, as the Royal Navy destroyer moved away, the explosions receded and the emerald aura grew fainter. When depth charges could no longer be heard reverberating through the submarine's hull, the mysterious light vanished.

UB-65 managed to surface and return to its home base, where once again a new crew were put aboard to replace those suffering nervous breakdowns.

UB-65 was last seen on the surface off the coast of Ireland, near Cape Clear. The submarine's final voyage occurred in July 1918, just four months before the Armistice was signed. On July 10, the captain of an American submarine patrolling at periscope depth was surprised to see an enemy U-boat resting motionless on the surface. There were no signs of life on her deck, nor was there any suggestion anyone was at her helm. She just bobbed in the ocean, unmoving, waves rocking her gently. She looked abandoned.

The American sailors couldn't believe their good fortune. The U-boat presented a perfect target. Torpedoes were armed, manhandled into their tubes and prepared to fire. Just when the skipper was about to give the order, he saw through his periscope a dark figure materialize on the bow of UB-65, arms folded, staring defiantly back at him. The skipper was momentarily taken aback. Just as training and duty kicked back in and he was about to order the torpedo launch, UB-65 suddenly and mysteriously exploded in a giant fireball. She went to her watery grave with her crew of 34 men and the trapped soul of the undead first officer. To this day, no one knows how the submarine exploded, nor why it had been sitting defenseless and presumably lifeless that day.

However, the vessel rises on certain stormy nights to prowl once more. Crews aboard several ships have been disturbed by her sudden appearance. Such echoes of her troubled past thankfully last only a few short minutes, after which the witnesses are relieved to see the U-boat slide beneath the waves once more. Is UB-65 forever tainted, or as time passes will the ocean currents eventually wash away her evil?

Cap Trafalgar, Ghost Ship of the South Atlantic

The oceans of the world are deep and mysterious, and they give up their secrets only reluctantly. Old sailors who have spent a lifetime at sea can regale listeners with tales of unexplained shipwrecks, terrible sea monsters, spectral vessels emerging from deep fog banks…all manner of strangeness that leaves a man questioning his sanity. Sailors are a superstitious lot, and it's no wonder. If you spend enough time at sea, you'll witness things—weird things that just can't be explained logically.

How does one explain, for example, the strange coincidences that surround the steamships *Cap Trafalgar* and *Carmania*? They met during the First World War under unusual circumstances. One has even spawned a ghost ship said to sail the South Atlantic to this day, engaged in a never-ending patrol even though there are no longer any enemy ships to be found.

During World War I, the German navy converted a number of merchant ships into disguised warships, or "Q-ships" as they were called by the British admiralty. Guns were concealed behind wooden flaps that could be raised in seconds to point their muzzles at surprised enemy vessels, and superstructures were altered to resemble known Allied merchant ships. The concept was that these Q-ships would be able to lure enemy merchant ships within shooting range under false colours, sending up their real flag only after the enemy had been fooled, and then order the ship to surrender. And it often worked; when war was declared in 1914, German Q-ships became the bane of the Royal Navy, sinking dozens of ships.

One of the ships altered by Germany was the ocean liner *Cap Trafalgar,* a majestic vessel built at the AG Vulcan Shipyard in Hamburg for the trans-Atlantic trade. She was a large ship, measuring 613 feet (187 metres) in length, 72 feet (22 metres) wide and weighing several thousand tons, yet she was still capable of sustained cruising at 17 knots. Completed in July 1913, *Cap Trafalgar* spent the next year steaming between Germany and ports in South America, where large numbers of German immigrants had settled.

August 1914 found her in South American waters. Prearranged plans indicated that in the event of the outbreak of war with Britain, she would be conscripted into military service and transformed into a disguised auxiliary cruiser. Immediately upon hearing that war had erupted in Europe, *Cap Trafalgar* hurriedly disembarked all passengers and non-essential personnel and then steamed off to rendezvous with the German warship SMS *Eber.*

When the two vessels met, a veteran naval officer, Korvetternkapitan (Lieutenant-Commander) Wirth came aboard *Cap Trafalgar* and took command from her peacetime skipper. He brought with him a core of naval officers to train the civilian crew, and whatever ammunition and stores *Eber* could spare. In addition, Wirth oversaw an at-sea refit to arm her with eight powerful guns and cleverly disguise her as the Allied ocean liner *Carmania.* Wirth's orders were to sink British ships wherever he could locate them throughout the South Atlantic.

Based on his orders, Wirth probably should have begun hunting down enemy ships immediately. Instead he decided to steer *Cap Trafalgar* toward a secret German naval base that had been established on the Brazilian island of Trindade, 800 kilometres east of the Brazilian mainland, where he hoped to bring aboard enough supplies to sustain a lengthy cruise. It was a fateful mistake.

On September 14, 1914, *Cap Trafalgar* was anchored at Trinidade, refuelling from two colliers, when a plume of smoke was seen rising on the horizon. The masquerading German warship emerged from its secret anchorage to confront its first target, which turned out to be a large ocean liner. Even while Wirth was calling his crew to action, he was confident of an easy victory. Here's where things get strange.

As the two vessels drew nearer, their respective crews were astounded to see that both ships were identical in appearance, even down to the name on their bows. *Cap Trafalgar* had stumbled upon the very ship she was impersonating—*Carmania*. Ironically, the British had secretly transformed *Carmania* into a disguised auxiliary cruiser as well, intending her to flush out German steamships in the South Atlantic. And on this morning, it had worked perfectly.

What are the odds of these two covert warships, each one the mirror image of the other, meeting in the vastness of the world's oceans? The odds seem so beyond statistical reckoning as to be all but impossible. Certainly sailors aboard both vessels were stunned to see their ship's twin bearing down on them with guns cleared for action. But there was no time for the crews to ponder the implausibility of such an encounter. A battle was looming, and only one *Carmania* would sail away from it. What remained to be seen was which ship would prevail: the authentic one or the imposter.

The two ships began to fire their guns at each other as quickly as the crewmen could load them. Soon, both vessels were obscured by clouds of smoke and massive spouts of water thrown up by shells missing the mark, making aiming difficult. The fighting raged for over two intense hours, with *Carmania* taking a severe punishment from all the shells crashed into her hull. Crewmembers were blown apart by the explosions, shredded by flying debris or thrown overboard by the concussive blasts. *Carmania*'s bridge was totally destroyed by shellfire, and a massive gash along her waterline caused heavy flooding in her hull. The ship was battered, and most aboard her were certain she was on her last legs.

The crew of *Carmania* fought for their lives on the South Atlantic in the early days of World War I, narrowly winning the battle with *Cap Trafalgar* and going on to survive the war.

However, as the range between the ships closed, *Carmania*'s guns began to do some damage as well. *Cap Trafalgar* was soon just as battered, and as shell after shell tore through her superstructure, uncontrollable fires broke out. Flames raced through the interior, gutting rooms and burning alive those sailors too wounded to escape the raging inferno. Which ship could take the most punishment?

The matter was finally decided when *Cap Trafalgar* began rolling over to port. A shell had struck home below the waterline and ruptured several compartments, and the ship was rapidly sinking. Lifeboats were hurriedly lowered into the water, and many sailors, desperate to escape the condemned ship, dove into the Atlantic. Although 279 sailors managed to escape before she went down, she became a metal coffin for 51 men, including Captain Wirth, who, in true naval fashion, went down with his ship.

But though she had won the battle, *Carmania* wasn't out of danger. She was shattered. Flooded and listing severely, with fires burning throughout, she was barely seaworthy. At this critical juncture, another German ship, SMS *Kronprinz Wilhelm*, arrived on the scene, seemingly to finish off the battered British ship. The captain and crew of *Carmania* braced for the worst. Then something incredible happened. *Kronprinz Wilhelm*'s captain, fearing a trap, turned his ship about and sailed away without firing a shot.

By that stroke of luck, *Carmania* survived and was taken to Gibraltar for repairs. She later supported the 1916 Gallipoli campaign, then spent the remainder of the war as a troopship. Her final war duty was to transport Canadian soldiers back from Europe after the Armistice.

The broken hull of *Cap Trafalgar* lies on the seabed where she was sunk by *Carmania,* but even the crushing weight of the ocean cannot prevent her from occasionally rising to the surface to sail once more. Spawned from the darkest depths of the ocean, tainted by death and battle, she is a cursed shadow of her previous self; her only purpose now is to destroy and terrify the living. All that was once good and noble about the ship is gone. *Cap Trafalgar* is now a ghost ship propelled by the hate of her unliving crew who reside within her dark hold, forever tormented by the grisly nature of their deaths.

Like the legendary *Flying Dutchman*, it's said that to see *Cap Trafalgar* is a bad omen. Such a sighting, sailors are convinced, foreshadows very bad luck aboard their ship and all but assures their own demise. Mysterious deaths befall sailors after spotting the cursed vessel, all manner of accidents and unexplainable incidents befoul their ships, and in the worst instances, an innocent ship sinks—swamped in a storm, run aground on rocks, rolled over by a rogue wave—shortly after crossing paths with the spectral warship.

Folklore describes the most sinister encounters with *Cap Trafalgar*. A dark fog settles over the water, muffling the ocean's churning waves. The gulls flying overhead suddenly disappear, and the air becomes still and heavy. Without warning, a dark shape looms ahead. An ocean liner, its hull worn and beaten, sails past. The badly damaged liner is seemingly adrift and appears in distress. The lower-ranking crewmembers aboard the witnessing ship cross themselves—something about the other ship seems eerily amiss—while on the bridge, the captain and his officers scratch their beards at the wildly dancing instruments and tense up, knowing that they are now sailing blind.

A short while later, everyone aboard is thrown from their feet as metal scrapes against rock and the deck shudders underneath them. The ship has run aground, and now water pours through the gash in her hull. The ship is doomed, and the sailors race for the lifeboats. As they lower the boats into the water, the looming liner emerges from the fog bank once again. She hovers nearby, her wraithlike crew lining its railings to enjoy the panic of the sailors aboard the sinking ship as they fight to survive. Then, slowly, fog tendrils wrap themselves around the liner like the arms of a great white kraken, and she disappears once more.

The oceans of the world are prowled by many vessels with no man at their helm and not a single living soul aboard. *Cap Trafalgar* is just one of a virtual fleet of ghost ships hiding within the vastness of the sea, but she may well be one of the more sinister of them. Left in her wake is a trail of human misery and death. It's said that ghost ships are given "life" by the intense emotions of those who died aboard them, and that the strength of these emotions determines how long the ships' spectral cruises will endure. Will the accursed crew of *Cap Trafalgar* ever find peace within their watery grave and allow their doomed vessel to finally rest undisturbed on the ocean floor? Or are they doomed to continue their cruise of terror for eternity?

Grave Premonitions

"We have to learn to look death in the face here and pass the time of day with him," wrote Canadian soldier Angus Martin in 1916. It was prophetic. Only a month later, he was killed in combat.

Death was ever present in World War I, and soldiers became eerily accustomed to it. They could walk past a bloated, rotting corpse without revulsion and barely notice the stomach-churning stench. Before going "over the top" to assault the enemy lines, they might shake the skeletal hand of a body protruding from the earthen wall of their trench, with grim humour asking the fallen soldier to "wish me luck, chap." A direct hit from a shell might obliterate all sign of a friend you were chatting with just moments before, wiping him from the face of the earth so completely it was as if he never existed. And it didn't miss any soldier's observation that the trenches criss-crossing the battlefield resembled long graves. Death wasn't merely a fact of life in the First World War; it was a constant companion.

Many men became so attuned to death that they experienced, and subsequently wrote about, uncanny visions offering a glimpse or sense of impending doom. With infantrymen often suffering 50 percent casualties in battle, it is not surprising that many of them felt their imminent demise before they went on the attack. But these premonitions were more than just a product of their knowledge that the odds were not in their favour. They were usually accompanied by ghostly visitors or supernatural visions that shed some light on the portending events. Sometimes, these visions would actually save a man's life.

Canadian soldier Frank Iriam described one such episode in his postwar writings: "When about 150 yards from the corner [of some elm groves], I seemed to sense or feel some impending evil, stopping and saying to my mate, wait a little, we will sit on that old log lying there for a few minutes and have a smoke. I felt that I was expecting something to happen. Sure enough, over came a five-point-nine-inch shell hitting directly on the path at the corner of that elm grove. Had we kept straight on we would have been just in time to connect with the shell."

What had caused Iriam to pause at the log? Was it some sort of psychic awareness, divine intervention or spiritual guidance? It's a question many soldiers who had similar experiences pondered.

Some men recorded experiences that went beyond mere premonitions to include apparitions, typically of distant or even deceased loved ones. One night, while carrying shells forward to the front lines, an unidentified soldier watched in horror as the horizon lit up with an eerie glow. Enemy artillery was beginning a deadly barrage. The soldier dropped his load and dove for cover in a shallow shell hole, where he began clawing the earth with his bare hands in a desperate attempt for more protection. Just as shells began to explode around him, he peered over the edge and saw the figure of his beloved mother standing only a short distance away. "I saw you looking towards me as plain as life," remembered the soldier in a letter written home a short time later.

Along with the tales of horror and hardship that came from the Western Front, came tales of miraculous and unexplained, life-saving premonitions and apparitions.

Dumbstruck, the soldier crawled toward his mother, reaching out to her, in the terror of the moment wanting nothing more than to feel her comforting embrace. Just as he reached the spot where her image had stood just moments prior, a German shell slammed into the hole he had just left behind and exploded with a deafening roar. "Had it not been for you, I certainly would have been reported 'missing,'" the soldier wrote. ("Missing," in this case, being a euphemism for being literally incinerated by the blast, leaving nothing to be buried.) "You'll turn up again, won't you, Mother, next time a shell is coming?"

Impossible appearances were numerous among the soldiers of the Great War. None, however, was more powerful than the experience of Canadian soldier William Bird.

Bird's moving account of the night his brother's ghost saved him is among the most famous paranormal events of the war. Bird, who had a postwar career as a respected journalist in Nova Scotia, published his wartime memoirs under the title *Ghosts Have Warm Hands*. His book is regarded by historians as one of the finest eyewitness accounts of the war; therefore, the spectral encounter he describes carries with it a great deal of weight.

The story is set in the aftermath of the April 1917 Battle of Vimy Ridge. Bird, then a corporal serving with the kilted 42nd Battalion, was a hardened combat veteran of over two years at the front. During his wartime service, Bird had become accustomed to terrible things—things that in his previous civilian life would have terrified him. The sound of bullets zipping past his head, the sight and smell of corpses rotting in the sun, and the sight of shell-fire tearing up the earth as well as soldiers had become commonplace. He had killed men, and men had attempted to kill him. He was a man not easily frightened or given to flights of fancy.

After a cold night on a working party where he oversaw the digging of trenches and laying of barbed wire, Bird was exhausted and chilled to the bone. He could think of nothing but lying down, pulling a blanket up under his chin and falling asleep. He stumbled through the labyrinth of trenches scarring the French landscape, uncertain as to where he would sleep, when he happened upon a shell hole with a tarp pegged over it to keep out the freezing rain pelting down from above. Bedded down in the hole were two soldiers from the neighbouring 73rd Battalion. Seeing the exhaustion in Bird's face, they took pity on him and offered to share their shelter. Bird gratefully accepted and slipped into a coma-like sleep almost immediately.

Before dawn, warm hands shook Bird's shoulders, stirring him from his deep slumber. Annoyed at being awoken so early after a long night of work, he tried to pull free, but the "grip held." Wiping away the sleep from his eyes, he looked with amazement at his brother Steve, reported "missing in action" in 1915, leaning over him with concern etched into his face. Still weary with exhaustion and only slowly recovering from the interruption of his deep sleep, it took Bird a few moments to realize something was wrong. Questions began to flood his foggy brain. Hadn't Steve been listed as "presumed killed" when he went missing? How had he survived? What was he doing here now? Why had his parents not written to him that Steve had escaped from a German prisoner-of-war camp? And how had Steve located him in the blasted expanse of the battlefield? Nothing made sense, but in his joy at seeing his brother once again, William pushed such questions aside.

Steve grinned as he released his grip, then put a warm hand over his brother's mouth as Will began to shout out his happiness. Steve gestured toward the others sleeping in the hole, as if reluctant to wake them. "Get your gear," he said softly, pointing to Will's rifle and equipment.

Drawing his still-groggy brother out of the shell hole and beckoning him to follow, Steve moved quickly across the shattered landscape, weaving his way around craters, the shredded stumps of trees and tangled barbed wire. The crumbling remains of a farmstead appeared in the pre-dawn mist. Steve led Will into the ruins, soundlessly scampering over mounds of brick and under fallen timbers.

He rounded a corner and then, to Will's astonishment, simply disappeared. There was nowhere he could have possibly gone. It was as if the earth had opened up and swallowed him whole.

Confused and distressed, Will searched for his brother. They had just been reunited, and he couldn't bear the thought of losing him again. But after a few desperate moments, the full weight of his loss came crushing down. Steve had never truly been there. He was dead and buried in some unmarked grave. Will realized that he must have been sleep-walking or hallucinating. There was no other explanation. Tears streaked down his face, and he suddenly felt overwhelming exhaustion; he was physically and emotionally spent. He collapsed into another shell hole and fell into a deep sleep.

Bird was awoken again in the harsh light of a new day by hands shaking his shoulders. His eyes fluttered open to reveal several of his friends standing over him. They were astonished and pleased to find him alive. Bird climbed out of his hole and shook away the sleep. Together, he and his fellow soldiers left the ruins behind to make their way back to their battalion.

Bird suddenly stopped short. There before him was the shell hole in which he had originally bedded down, the one from which Steve had lured him away. He was horrified to see that it had been destroyed by a direct hit from a high-explosive shell. The other soldiers, the two who had graciously offered to share their shelter with Bird, had been dismembered beyond all recognition. There was so little remaining of them that other soldiers were trying to sift through the viscera to determine if they could bury a few of the body parts together or if they would all just be scooped together into a sand bag for burial.

Bird became highly emotional. The realization that he too would have been killed if not for the intervention of his deceased brother left him shaken. He had never before given much thought to the existence of spirits, but he knew now that ghosts were very real. The experience had been so vivid, and his survival so unlikely otherwise, that it left no doubt in his mind.

Like many people who have had seen a ghost, Bird recounted his supernatural experience sparingly to his fellow soldiers, self-consciously aware that he sounded deranged and worried that they would lose confidence in him. He did, however, write about it extensively and openly in postwar years, and he went to his grave absolutely convinced that his deceased brother had returned, if only in spirit form, to save him from a grisly death. Nothing anyone could say would sway him from his steadfast belief in the existence of ghosts and the paranormal.

Few soldiers who had life-changing visions while serving in the trenches spent much time speculating as to the visions' origins. They were simply accepted as part of a soldier's sixth sense, that intuition veteran soldiers acquire that sees their ears attuned to the scream of incoming shells, where one recognizes the location of a sniper all but invisible to the human eye, and where muscle memory reacts faster than the brain can transmit orders. Experienced soldiers in all wars seem to develop such survival instincts.

But it's also possible that in some cases, soldiers were indeed saved by a supernatural presence, their lives spared by the apparition of a fallen compatriot or a remembered loved one. It's often said that once the bullets start to fly, a soldier isn't fighting for his country but for the man beside him and his family back home. We don't think it's unlikely that the bonds between soldiers and their loved ones might extend beyond the parameters of logic to cheat death of yet another victim.

Longleat

It seems that Sir John Alexander Thynne, a young man and member of the British aristocracy who was killed in action in France in 1916 while leading his soldiers on the front lines, is somehow lost between worlds. His former home, Longleat, a palatial estate in Wiltshire, England, has been in his family since the Reformation, so it's no wonder that when the young man returned to this plane in death, he did so to the house he once called home. Spectral activity associated with him has been reported most frequently in the Red Library of the manor. It's as if Sir John sits, trying to read, as thousands of tourists flock year after year through his sanctuary. The very warmth and beauty that lured his spirit back to Longleat from the grave also lures gawking visitors, thereby preventing him from finding the solace he deserves. Disappointed that his peace is intruded upon, Sir John acts out in a variety of harmless but nonetheless startling ways.

Longleat became the first of Britain's stately homes to be open to the public in 1949. Very few places conjure up a more vivid image of the English aristocracy than this one, home of the Thynne family for 13 generations. Amazing history that spans 450 years can only add to the inexplicable events, superstitions, legends and ghostly activities. Sir John Alexander Thynne isn't the only spirit in residence within these gilded halls, and he's the youngest by centuries. Indeed, the estate's best-known ghost stories centre upon the young soldier's more illustrious ancestors.

One of the most famous and sinister legends surrounding Longleat is that of Lady Louisa Carteret, the wife of Sir Thomas Thynne, 2nd Viscount of Weymouth (1710–1751). Lady Louisa was young and beautiful, but she was unhappy. She was lonely and craved attention from her husband, who had eyes only for accumulating more power and wealth.

Loneliness and the burden of an unhappy marriage eventually caught up to Lady Louisa. When her devoted footman showed her the attention she craved, her good judgement failed her. The two became passionate lovers. Although they tried to be discrete, it wasn't long before their affair was the talk of the manor.

For a time, the Viscount was oblivious to the hushed talk of his servants, but eventually, he began to take notice. Finally, Thomas discovered what all the whispering was about and wasted no time in confronting his wife, then brutally punishing her lover. When all his rage had been spent, there was nothing remaining of the footman but a bloody, broken corpse. The only thing left to do was to dispose of it. Adding insult to injury, instead of giving the young man a proper burial, he simply placed the body beneath a flagstone in the basement. It was a bold statement: the servant had been nothing more than dirt under his shoe, someone he could literally walk upon.

Lady Louisa knew her lover had been punished, likely beaten, but she had no idea that Thomas was so cruel as to kill the man. Certain her husband had imprisoned her lover, she took to searching the rooms of the house in hopes of finding her faithful servant and true love, oblivious that his body was now lying in the cold ground beneath the basement. This would forever be Lady Louisa's punishment: to mourn the loss of the man who for a short time gave her the love and attention she never received from her husband. Never getting over the loss of her lover, young Lady Louisa let herself slowly die of a broken heart, which finally stopped beating on Christmas Day, 1736.

As decades passed, the story became legend. Many people began to believe that the tale of the ill-fated lovers was nothing more than folklore. Then, in the early 20th century, when central heating was being installed at Longleat, workers had to lower the floor in the basement in order to fit in the new boiler. They were shocked at what they discovered when they put shovel to earth. There, in a shallow grave beneath the stones, lay a human skeleton. The story was true after all.

Today, Louisa is the "Green Lady" of Longleat, a beautiful ghost said to wander, grief stricken and wretched, along the corridor that now carries her name, in hopes of being reunited with her lover. But she certainly isn't the only ghost at Longleat. The spectre of Sir John Thynne, the home's original owner, is also often encountered within the manor's lavish halls. He was the first master of Longleat, and he doesn't seem willing to accept that it's no longer his to lord over.

Sir John was a remarkably strong-willed, driven man who, over a 40-year period, worked his way up from Master of the Kitchen for King Henry VIII to one of the richest, most powerful nobles in the land. Hard work, not birthright or patronage, was behind the success that gave him a position of social power and great wealth. In 1540, during Henry VIII's Dissolution of the Monasteries (when the English king abolished Catholic monasteries and sold off their holdings), Sir John paid the then-princely sum of

53 pounds to acquire a tumble-down former monastery. On these holy grounds he set about building a magnificent country home that would reflect his wealth and status, transforming the monastery into the lavish estate that we admire today. The house has remained in the possession of his descendants ever since, and many generations have left their mark on it.

Buried in 1580, Sir John Thynne has been unable to give up his residence. Perhaps because of his cruelty, the murdering husband does not rest easy in his grave. Still believing that the building belongs to him, he roams the halls in a vain effort to deter visitors from lingering too long. Nevertheless, though he was an unlikable and dangerous man and likes to startle the living with his sudden manifestations, he seems harmless enough. A young child who once spotted him merely wondered who the old man was who had somehow walked through a wall. She was curious, but hardly frightened. If you want to meet the original lord of the manor, make your way down to the Red Library. That's where his wispy form is most often seen.

The elderly apparition shares the library with a much younger spirit, ironically enough his namesake, John Alexander Thynne, who died in action during World War I. Tour guides have seen the younger ghost casually reading books in the library and have mistaken him for a visitor. When approached, he simply fades from view. But he's never gone long, always returning again to the home in which he was raised.

John Alexander Thynne, 8th Viscount of Weymouth, was born in 1895. He was the son of a very prominent man, Sir Thomas Thynne, 5th Marquess of Bath and 7th Viscount of Weymouth, a longtime Member of Parliament who at one time held the prestigious post of Under-Secretary of State for India. John Alexander was the eldest son and heir and, with his father's influence, almost certainly could have either avoided military service when war broke out or been assigned to a comfortable, safe posting. But he came from a long line of soldiers and was raised to believe strongly in the concept of duty and obligation to one's country. A young man of honour, John Alexander could not in good conscience avoid combat knowing someone else would have to fight in his place.

When World War I erupted, he enlisted in the army as a second lieutenant in the 2nd Dragoons (Royal Scots Greys), a proud cavalry regiment. Tragically, his honour was his undoing. He died on February 13, 1916, at Pas de Calais while leading his men in battle. But though he died in France, John Alexander's spirit returned home to Longleat.

His mother, the Marchioness, often had visions that foretold tragedy or some kind of looming disaster, and she actually "saw" the death of her eldest son the day before it happened. This eerie prediction was heralded by another of Longleat's long-held superstitions: that the Thynnes are doomed to die out if the swans, which have nested on the grounds for centuries, should fly away. That particular day, February 12, 1916, the Marchioness had seen one of the swans fly away from the house and disappear into the distance. Shaken by the ominous event, she then had the vision of her beloved son's death. She became hysterical, sobbing uncontrollably for hours on end, and there was nothing either her husband or her servants could say that would convince her that her son would be all right. When the news arrived of John Alexander's death, the already fragile woman fell into a deep depression.

Perhaps John Alexander returned to Longleat to console his grieving, despondent mother. It's a comforting thought. But what's certain is that his spirit has been there ever since and has been seen by numerous eyewitnesses—family, staff and tourists alike—over the past century.

Jean Alpin, a longtime tour guide at Longleat, had several encounters with the spiritual residents during her decades of leading tourists through the stately home. One memorable experience took place on November 8, 1984, in the Red Library. "At about three in the afternoon I was taking a small group of visitors around the house. When I opened the door to the Red Library, I was surprised to see the room was already occupied. A man was standing behind a desk; he was tall, dark haired and young," she recalled.

The young man was reading a book and didn't look up when Jean and her tour group entered. In fact, he showed no sign of noticing them whatsoever. Normally, as is guide's practice when encountering someone unescorted within the estate, Jean would have approached the stranger and asked him his business. But she didn't. Something about his bearing told her that he had every right to be there, and he looked oddly familiar to her. Thinking the young man was perhaps an extended member of the Thynne family, Jean left him alone. She instead turned her attention back to the tour group, leading them back out into the hall on their way to the next room. When she glanced over her shoulder into the library a few moments later, the mysterious young man was gone.

Jean thought nothing of it. She simply assumed he had made a discreet exit while she was otherwise occupied sharing with the tour group some of Longleat's rich history. It was only later in the tour that it suddenly dawned on her who she had encountered in the library. She was in the Breakfast Room, talking to the group about the family portraits hanging on the wall, when she recognized the face of the young man from the library. Looking at one of the portraits, Jean realized the man she had seen was in fact John Alexander Thynne, the current owner's elder brother.

"I remember thinking to myself, 'Oh, that's all right then, that's who it was,' and still the penny hadn't dropped. It was not until I got down to the Lower Dining Room that it suddenly hit me. John Alexander had died in action in 1916," she says, absolutely convinced about the identity of the library's visitor. "He was not ghostly in any sense, but very real. I was not frightened because at the time he looked just as real as any of the people in my party. I don't know if any of them saw him. I can still recall the strong feeling I had that he was related to Lord Bath."

It had been Jean's first experience with the spirits of Longleat, but it wouldn't be her last. Over her years working in the stately home, she has had several encounters with long-dead members of the Thynne family. But she's never been afraid, reasoning that they have more right to be in their home than she or the members of the public do.

Ask anyone who has ever spent any time at Longleat, and most have little doubt that John Alexander Thynne still wanders through the building a century after his passing, enjoying the manor's comforts as he did while he was alive. If you work in the building long enough, you'll eventually meet the man himself—in one form or another. Sometimes it's a subtle meeting characterized by mysterious noises coming from an empty room or a door swinging shut without any prompting from human hands. Other times, however, introductions to Thynne are more startling.

On more than one occasion, a person has been stunned to come face to face with a smartly dressed young man who seems distinctly out of time and place. Most frequently the ghost is seen in the Red Library, but encounters have taken place in other chambers. Moments after being stumbled upon, he simply fades away, leaving the eyewitness alone and struggling to catch his breath after the unsettling experience.

Ever since it opened its doors to the public for guided tours, Longleat has proved an irresistible draw to visitors from all over the world. Who can resist an opportunity to walk through British history, to peak behind the curtains into the lives of the nobility and marvel at the wealth and splendour? So welcoming are its elegant corridors, beautifully decorated rooms and manicured gardens that former, never mind dead, residents are equally drawn to Longleat. For them, it is quite literally home.

Lawrence of Arabia

In 1925, T.E. Lawrence, best remembered by the world today as the legendary Lawrence of Arabia, purchased a quaint, white-washed cottage called Cloud's Hill, near Bovington, in Dorset. While simple, the cottage had undeniable rustic charm, with exposed beams in its rooms, handmade furnishings that demonstrated the craftsmanship of the carpenter, an open hearth and a surrounding hedge of rhododendrons with brilliant blooms the size of dinner plates.

Lawrence loved this rural cottage. It was his sanctuary, a place where he could escape his fame and find peace. It was only there that he felt at home. In May 1935, Lawrence wrote about Cloud's Hill to a friend, Nancy Astor, proclaiming, "Nothing would take me away. It is an earthly paradise, and I am staying here."

Five days later, he was fatally injured in a motorcycle accident. But the sentiment expressed in the letter proved prophetic. His ghost, often adorned in the swirling white Arab robes for which he was famed, has often been seen within the cottage. He was right. Nothing, not even death, would take him away from Cloud's Hill.

Thomas Edward Lawrence was born on August 16, 1888, at Tremadoc, Caernarvonshire, in Wales, the second of five illegitimate sons of Sir Thomas Chapman by his daughters' governess, Sara Maden. Lawrence was educated at Oxford, and in the five years prior to World War I, he visited the Middle East on several occasions to prepare material for his university thesis on the architecture of crusader castles. His visits to the Middle East weren't all academic in nature, however. A 1914 expedition to the Sinai led by Captain S.F. Newcombe and Leonard Woolley, which Lawrence accompanied and whose purpose was ostensibly to explore and map the area, was in reality designed to gain information for the British War Office about Turkish military dispositions on the Turkish-Egyptian border.

Owing to his considerable knowledge of the Middle East, when war broke out in 1914, Lawrence was sent to Egypt and attached to the military intelligence staff concerned with Arab affairs. He couldn't have known at the time that he would play a pivotal role in the war against the German-allied Ottoman Empire.

In October 1916, Lawrence accompanied a mission to the Hejaz, where the Arabs had proclaimed a revolt against the Turks. The following month, the young officer was ordered to join the Arab forces as a political and liaison officer. Lawrence identified strongly with the Arab cause and was instrumental in acquiring large quantities of military assistance from the British army for their rebellion against the Turks. Determined to make the Arab revolt a real contribution to an Allied victory over the Central Powers, he gave new life to an insurrection that then had little momentum and no direction by securing additional supplies and providing clear and attainable strategic goals.

It was Lawrence, for example, who identified that the Ottoman Empire's control of the Middle East lay in the Damascus–Medina railway. This railway was the link between cities and forts isolated by inhospitable desert, and the means by which the Turks could send reinforcements to crush the Arab revolt. Under Lawrence's direction, the Arabs began a series of guerrilla attacks on the railway designed to disrupt its operation. Later, he led an Arab force that captured the vital Red Sea port of Aqaba on July 6, 1917, and he was also present at the Battle of Tafila in January 1918. For his conduct there, he was promoted to lieutenant-colonel.

Lawrence's contribution to the successful outcome of the First World War was considerable: his advice and influence allied the Arabs to the British cause, thereby tying down at least 25,000 Turkish troops that would otherwise have been opposed to the British army. His exploits in the desert were legendary, earning him the name Lawrence of Arabia. But it should be pointed out that he was never actually a leader of the Arab forces—command always remained firmly in the hands of the Arabs themselves.

In the postwar period, Lawrence came to resent his fame. It haunted him, invaded upon his privacy and led to expectations among an adoring public that he could never hope to meet. As a result, he was forced to live under a succession of assumed names. He enlisted in the Royal Air Force in 1922 under the name of John Hume Ross. When his real identity was discovered a few months later, he resigned. In February 1923, he enlisted in the Royal Tank Corps under the name of Thomas Edward Shaw, but once again was found out and forced to leave. Finally, reluctantly, he accepted that there was no escaping his fame and once again joined the Royal Air Force in 1925, this time under his real name. As a pilot, Lawrence was able to indulge his passion for speed and excitement.

By the time the war ended, Lawrence of Arabia was one of the most famous men in Britain—and is now one of that country's most famous ghosts.

That same year, Lawrence purchased Cloud's Hill, a small cottage in Dorset. He found contentment in its tranquil setting. It was there that he finished his wartime memoirs, *The Seven Pillars of Wisdom*, in 1926. It was also there that he entertained his many famous friends, including authors Thomas Hardy, George Bernard Shaw and E.M. Forster.

In 1935, Lawrence left the air force and retired to Cloud's Hill. To fulfill a need for thrills, he took to riding his motorcycle at reckless speeds along the winding roads of the Dorset countryside. It was while enjoying his new retirement that he wrote his letter to Lady Astor about the solace the cottage offered, including his prophetic statement, "Nothing would take me away."

On May 13, five days after penning that letter, Lawrence started his motorcycle and, with a roar, a plume of smoke and a spray of gravel, headed off down the country lane. The wind in his face and the thrum of the machine was exhilarating. Smiling broadly, he pushed the motorcycle to greater speeds. He had never felt more alive.

Rounding a corner at speed, his smile left instantly and his eyes grew wide. Directly ahead in his path were two young boys on their bicycles. There was no time to brake. Lawrence could do nothing but swerve sharply in a desperate bid to avoid the startled youngsters. The barrelling motorcycle missed the boys, but there was no time for Lawrence to feel a sense of relief. A split second later, he was airborne. He screamed in terror. Then, both he and his motorcycle fell silent as they crashed into a tree with a sickening thud and lay in a twisted heap on the ground.

An ambulance from the nearby Bovington Army Camp Hospital raced to the scene. Arriving at the crash site, the attendants were horrified at the state in which they found Lawrence. They gingerly slid his body onto a litter and placed him in the back of the ambulance for a race against time to the hospital. Lawrence was rushed into surgery, where doctors worked to save the legend's life, but sadly, their efforts were in vain. He died six days later, on May 19, 1935.

Perhaps trying to outrun his fame, Lawrence rode his motorcycle at reckless speeds, and it eventually cost him his life.

T.E. Lawrence's funeral was held in the church in Moreton, not far from Cloud's Hill, on May 21, 1935. Hundreds of friends and admirers turned up for the event, mourning the loss of a national hero. The nation was still grieving when, only a few short weeks later, the ethereal figure of Lawrence of Arabia was first seen entering his beloved cottage at dusk. Despair at the tragic and shocking nature of his death has led to an unnatural shackling of Lawrence's spirit to the mortal world. Where else would he return to than his beloved cottage?

Cloud's Hill is today maintained by the National Trust and is open for viewing, enabling the public to experience first hand the atmosphere that initially drew Lawrence there, and that keeps his ghost bound to the property decades after his death. Downstairs, the cottage has a tiny kitchen and an adjacent bedroom, not much bigger, its walls lined with books. Climbing the narrow stairs, each well-worn floorboard creaking with age, visitors enter a large room, where Lawrence entertained his famous guests. Most who explore the cottage immediately sense the same welcoming calmness that attracted Lawrence. Others, however, feel something else—something amiss. They feel Lawrence's restless presence, and some of them even see the legendary figure himself.

A ghostly figure in the flowing white Arabic dress that Lawrence wore in the desert has been reported within, or more frequently, entering, the cottage. Rarely is the apparition seen at the height of day. Most often, the spirit emerges to float around the cottage as the shadows deepen at dusk.

On the rare occasions in which Lawrence's spectral echo comes face to face with daytime visitors, it leaves them shaken and anxious to leave. The famously welcoming cottage suddenly doesn't feel welcoming any longer. Lawrence's shimmering shade chills the blood of those who see him, for the transparency of his form leaves little doubt that he is not of this world. He locks eyes with the visitor, his cold, penetrating gaze conveying his disapproval. It's apparent that he resents the intrusion on his privacy. Then, with a sweep of his white robes, he turns and drifts slowly away, fading into nothingness as he goes.

Multiple people have heard disembodied voices and footsteps in the cottage. But one American tourist, Todd Martin, experienced something more unusual and equally inexplicable. "When we entered the house, the batteries in my camera drained, though I had placed fresh batteries in it the evening before. I replaced the batteries with another fresh set and was able to shoot about 15 pictures before the new set of batteries drained," he explains. "With no more batteries, I tried to take some pictures with my cellphone, but it was frozen. You know where this is going; as soon as I left the cottage, the phone re-booted and worked fine."

In life, Lawrence was a free spirit, and in death, he's no different. His ghost is not confined to Cloud's Hill. An apparition wearing his distinctive white robes has been reported in the hospital where he died. Although his face is never seen, there is no doubt in anyone's mind of the identity of the fleeting ghost. His spectral figure is also said to make occasional appearances at the Wareham Museum, which has a collection of his memorabilia on display.

The cemetery at Moreton, where Lawrence is buried, is very old, dating back centuries. Many of the gravestones are cracked and tilted. And a lot of people say the place is haunted. Some of them have sworn to have seen Lawrence's spectre standing over his tombstone, gazing down at his grave as if contemplating what his life could have been if only it wasn't cut short by his reckless thrill-seeking. Hundreds of people visit Lawrence's gravesite every year; some are admirers, others are avid ghost hunters hoping to witness the heroic wraith. A single red rose is often mysteriously left on his grave—no one knows by whom.

Nicole was visiting the cemetery one winter's day to pay her respects to her grandfather when she had a startling encounter with Lawrence's spirit. "It had snowed during the night, just enough to leave a thin, powdery cover over the ground. My shoes crunched over the patchy snow as I walked to my grandfather's grave," she explains. "I was kneeling at the grave, placing some flowers against the stone, when I heard snow crunching somewhere behind me. I looked up to see who else was in the cemetery but saw no one. I was alone."

Or so she thought. Nicole turned her attention back to her grandfather, and soon after that, the sounds of footfalls crunching through the snow began again. She quickly turned her head to the right and saw a man striding through the headstones perhaps 50 metres away.

"He was a gentleman, middle-aged, tall and slender, dressed in a kind of suit, or perhaps a military uniform. What I remember most was the fact he had no legs. Below the waist he was a writhing mass of what I can only describe as smoke or mist. I didn't get a great look because he faded away after a second or two," Nicole explains. "I didn't believe in ghosts, but there one was. I mustered up enough courage to go over to where the ghost was when it disappeared. There were fresh footprints in the snow leading right up to the grave of Lawrence of Arabia, but when I tried to follow them back to their source, they disappeared after a short distance." Nicole believes it was Lawrence's ghost she saw that day, visiting his own gravesite.

There's one final location where Lawrence's roving spectre has been seen. In a ghostly echo of the moments leading up to his horrific crash, the unmistakable roar of a ghostly motorcycle still sounds on local Dorset roads, usually in the hours before dawn, hurtling along the country lanes at break-neck speeds. Those familiar with antique motorcycles have said that the sound of Lawrence's model of cycle—the Brough Superior—is unmistakable and is not easily confused with any other vehicle. These experts assert that the roar witnesses claim to hear is distinctly that of a Brough Superior.

Many people who reside in the vicinity of Cloud's Hill have seen a single, mysterious light piercing the darkness in the dead of night, moving rapidly along the roads like a speeding will-o'-the-wisp. Is this the headlight of Lawrence's ethereal motorcycle as he speeds down the winding rural lanes? Most people with an open mind believe so. Is Lawrence doomed to relive his ill-fated ride for all eternity, or might he return home safely to his cottage one black night and then be allowed to cross over to the other side for a more restful afterlife?

The south of England is an area steeped in mystery. From the two great stone temples at Avebury and Stonehenge, to the strange figures and white horses carved into the chalk hillsides, to the massive earthworks said to be the work of the devil—it's a place that stirs the imagination. Normally, a modest white-washed cottage wouldn't deserve mention in the same breath as those great mystical landmarks. But when that cottage belonged to T.E. Lawrence, better known to the world as the larger-than-life Lawrence of Arabia, and when stories are told that his robe-garbed spirit haunts the cottage to this day, suddenly what at first glance might appear to be a humble, nondescript building takes on epic proportions.

It was in that tiny cottage that Lawrence found the peace that eluded him so long in life. It's therefore ironic, and sad, that his love for the cottage has such a pull on him that it prevents him from finding peace in the afterlife.

Death from Above

For the first time in history, during the First World War, nations and their militaries were forced to face the threat of attack from the air. It was an entirely new danger, something only ever dreamed of in science fiction prior to the war. No threat presented a greater danger than Germany's massive Zeppelins, hydrogen-filled airships as long as a football field capable of carrying dozens of bombs.

Hot-air balloons had been used in warfare for decades, but because they had almost no lifting power and were completely at the mercy of the wind, they were used for little more than aerial observation of the battlefield. Author Jules Verne conceived of a balloon capable of directional flight in his 1886 novel *Robur the Conqueror* and its 1904 sequel *Master of the World*, but these books were viewed as mere science fiction stories, and the ideas in them were not taken seriously by either military men or civilian populations. The prescience of Verne's prediction, and the reality of air power, was demonstrated in June 1908 with the launch of Germany's first Zeppelin. Although appearing clumsy and unwieldy, these massive dirigibles could travel hundreds of kilometres at speeds almost as fast as the primitive airplanes of the day, and they could carry several tons of bombs, which could then be dropped on defenceless cities. People in Britain felt vulnerable, realizing that the English Channel would no longer isolate them from the ravages of a war in Europe.

These fears were realized seven years later when the first-ever aerial attacks against Britain occurred on the night of January 19–20, 1915, six months into World War I. That night, Zeppelins L3 and L4 were directed toward the Humber River but were driven off course by strong winds and instead dropped 24 bombs on Great Yarmouth, Sheringham, King's Lynn and surrounding villages. Four people were killed in the blasts, 16 injured, and more than a dozen buildings were destroyed or heavily damaged. The following month saw an attack upon London's docks, but Zeppelin commanders were under strict orders not to target residential areas of the city.

In May 1915, the German Kaiser, after months of intense pressure from his military commanders, finally—and very reluctantly—gave approval for the bombing of residential and commercial areas of the British capital. Even so, he placed restrictions on the raids. Most notably, he refused to allow the more affluent areas of London to be attacked. Bombs could be dropped only east of the Tower of London, among working class neighbourhoods. Enthused that the leashes holding them back had finally been slackened, the Army Airship Service prepared to bring the war to the British people.

After an intensive month of raids carried out across southeast England, on the evening of May 31, the dreaded Zeppelins finally descended upon London. The honour of this historic moment fell to Hauptman Erich Linnarz, a veteran of the Army Airship Service and commander of Zeppelin LZ38.

Around dusk on that May evening, LZ38 was towed out of her enormous, cocoon-like hangar at a base just north of Brussels, in occupied Belgium. She resembled a gleaming silver torpedo, thought Linnarz with admiration.

And like a torpedo, she was deadly. Teams of ground crew held fast her mooring lines as the Zeppelin drifted slightly in the wind. Linnarz and his crew boarded the airship and prepared for the historic flight. LZ38's engines sputtered to life, and on command, the ground crew released the mooring lines. The throb of the engines increased in pitch, and the massive props threatened to whisk away the caps of the men below. She was slowly lifting skyward for her maiden flight over London.

As the Zeppelin soared over the English Channel, Linnarz found it difficult to temper the excitement of the moment. Every member of the crew felt it. Finally, they would strike at the heart of the enemy. Excited faces peered through the forward window of the airship, eager to catch the first glimpse of London in the distance. They were supremely confident of success. The night was dark, with no moon, and they were certain their Zeppelin would remain undetected as it passed over England.

Residents of London were completely unaware of the danger heading in their direction. It was now almost 10 months since Britain had declared war on Germany, and the long-feared Zeppelin attack on London had not materialized. The raids at East Anglia, Essex and Kent had little effect on Londoners. Although the streets remained under black-out order, most people went about their lives as normal. The war, even the threat of bombs raining down from above, seemed distant. Londoners were about to be violently shaken from their complacency.

Around 11:00 PM, the London Metropolitan Police received notification of a pending raid against the city. While they were still absorbing the unexpected news,

LZ38 arrived and began to drop bombs on civilians lying in their beds.

Moments earlier, high above, Linnarz had looked down upon the sprawl of the sleeping city. The gentle hum of the Zeppelin's motors was soothing, and his previous excitement had been replaced by calm determination. Linnarz smiled tightly and plotted the path he would take. This night wouldn't be about hitting important facilities, such as dockyards or factories. It would be about spreading terror among the people, and he planned his course accordingly. The Zeppelin passed slowly over Stoke Newington High Street before turning and heading south, directly on a line leading toward the Tower of London, parallel with the Stoke Newington road. The airship dropped a heavy stream of bombs along the way, leaving behind a trail of devastation and fires to mark its passage.

The first bomb to crash down onto London, an incendiary designed to ignite fires, fell just south of a railway station onto the home of a humble clerk, Albert Lovell. It smashed through the roof, setting fire to two bedrooms on the top floor. The bewildered Mr. Lovell, his wife, children and two guests stumbled from the house without injury.

Not everyone would be so lucky that night. The bombing run lasted 20 minutes. The London Fire Brigade fought 41 fires, while members of the public extinguished others with buckets of water. Seven buildings were completely destroyed, and dozens more damaged. The Fire Brigade recorded the material damage for the night at 18,596 pounds. Seven people were killed. Crowds of stunned onlookers gathered in the streets throughout the bombed area, many brought to tears by the devastation and loss. There was no panic, but the sense of fear, sorrow and even hopelessness was tangible.

The British government hoped to inspire Londoners following the first air raids by German Zeppelins.

The raid, though brief, shook Londoners' morale. The airship LZ38 had been almost unseen as it passed over their city. Certainly no searchlights found her as she slowly glided overhead, and no guns or planes attacked her. There could be no hiding the fact: a Zeppelin had passed freely over London and, facing no opposition, had bombed civilian targets at will before departing without a single shot fired in return. No longer did the Londoners feel secure. War had come to their city, in the most terrifying manner imaginable.

Nevertheless, most people were rather quickly able to put the terrifying experience behind them, reasoning it was just one more terrible moment in a war full of them. Not everyone was able to move ahead so easily.

Samuel Leggatt was a widower. He lived on Cowper Road in London with his five children, doing his best to both provide for them by working long hours and also to nurture them as a mother would do. On the night of May 31, 1915, Leggatt was asleep in one room of his modest townhome while his children slept together in another. Suddenly, he was torn from his sleep. Light and heat enveloped him, and he felt his body leave the bed. He had a notion of screams echoing in the night as he spun, crashed into a wall and bounced off, twisting sideways now and slamming onto his shoulder. He ended up on his back, staring at the night sky through a cavernous hole in his roof. Although he was disoriented for several seconds, soon his head stopped spinning and the ringing in his ears subsided enough for him to realize that his house had been hit by a bomb, but that the explosion had now ceased.

Brick and wood and fragments of furnishings rained down on him as he sat up, stunned. His ears were still ringing, but he could hear the cries of "fire!" and "the Germans are here!" from the street outside his shattered window. Nearer, Leggatt heard his children screaming in terror. His nose twitched. There was smoke in the air. His home was on fire.

Leggatt jumped up and raced out into the hallway. The scene there was one of utter devastation. Plaster littered the hall, walls had collapsed, and black smoke was coiling out from the children's room. Leggatt fought his way into the room, suffering burns to his face and hands, but scooped up two of his terrified children. Arms full, he raced down the stairs and was met halfway by neighbours who had rushed over to lend a hand. Passing off the children to one of his neighbours, he and another man raced back upstairs to rescue the remaining three. By the time Leggatt and the neighbour burst through the door, the room was entirely engulfed in choking smoke that stung their eyes and throats. It was almost impossible to see or breathe. Flames by now were also racing into the room. The two men, groping through smoke and fire, desperately sought the children. Then, with the inferno chasing them out, they fled the building. From the safety of the street, they watched as the home was consumed by fire.

After having his burns tended to, Leggatt went to check on his children to ensure they were all right. He found them crying and in shock, but worst of all, he found them one short. In the confusion and smoke, he and his neighbour had each found one child and assumed the other man had found the other two children; in reality, each man had found and rescued only one child. Little Elsie, three years old and all freckles and curls, was missing. Police later discovered her burnt body under the bed, where she had crawled to hide from the fire.

Samuel Leggatt never truly put that night behind him. How could he? It had cost him one of his beloved children. And just as the painful wound started to heal, the little girl returned as a wispy apparition—still adorable with her round cheeks and playful smile, but now deathly pale—to remind him of his loss and tear open the wound anew. If only Leggatt could have wrapped his arms around her just one more time, pull her into a tight hug and tell her that he would always love her. Perhaps then they both could have found some peace. But of course that was impossible.

Leggatt found himself wishing he could stay awake all night to avoid the haunting dreams that were a constant reminder of his loss. Tears welled in his eyes whenever Elsie made one of her nighttime appearances, or when she would playfully announce her presence my mischievously hiding objects. His life after Elsie perished was a sad one. After all, can a parent ever truly recover from the death of a child, especially one so young and helpless?

Even after Leggatt himself was dead and gone, residents occasionally saw a young girl in white on the second floor of the house. She was a playful spirit, skipping happily along the hallway, playing peek-a-boo from around corners and under beds and tugging on people's clothing only to disappear as the target of the prank turned to look. In life, Elsie had the youthful charm that made everyone want to scoop her up, and death had done nothing to make her any less adorable. Eyewitnesses agreed the tiny ghost had chubby cheeks, curly hair, big, round eyes and a bubbly giggle. If you had to have a ghost plaguing your home, little Elsie would be most people's choice.

Unfortunately, she wasn't the only spectral reminder of that horrific night in 1915. There also seemed to be a psychic residue, likely caused by the anguish and terror of the Zeppelin attack, that caused echoes of that evening. Loud, unexplained noises coming from the upper floor in the middle of the night were routine occurrences that would startle people awake. These mysterious sounds included breaking glass, footsteps running across the floorboards and sudden, sharp crashes that sounded like furniture was being thrown about and overturned. It was chaos, and until residents grew accustomed to the noise, it frightened them because it sounded like intruders had broken in and were vandalizing the home. When they realized it was simply a residue of the past, the home-owners would simply lie in bed with blankets pulled up tight until the racket faded away.

Other times, the distinct smell of smoke would hang in the air. Searching the building top to bottom would reveal no flames or wisps of smoke that could cause the scent, and sure enough, after a time, the odour would simply fade. Finally, at any time of day, residents might hear unexplained noises (less startling than the nighttime racket, but puzzling nonetheless) and feel as though someone was there, watching them.

Much in London has changed since the last ghostly reports associated with the Leggatt house surfaced in the 1960s, let alone since the bombs fell on the unsuspecting city in 1915. Do energy and spirits linger still? Or has little Elsie found peace at long last? We hope she has.

Mysteries of the Mad Monk

Grigory Yefimovich Novych, the man better known to history as Rasputin, is a figure shrouded in mystery, intrigue, conspiracy theories and dark legends. A monk and mystic, he was also reputed to be a murderer, sorcerer and chronic womanizer—his moniker of Rasputin literally means "debauched one" in Russian, an offensive name implying a character whose sole interests were sex and alcohol. Russia's so-called "Mad Monk" remains one of the most enigmatic historical figures.

Born in January 1869, Rasputin was the son of Siberian peasants. The underprivileged Grigory received little formal education and spent much of his youth stealing and drinking. But despite his lack of schooling and his alcoholism, he was no fool and from an early age was fascinated by spiritualism and religion.

The young Siberian entered a monastery, where he fell under the influence of the controversial Skopsty sect, a cult whose members believed that to receive God's blessing one must first sin, claiming that otherwise there can be no cause for God's forgiveness. This doctrine fit well with Rasputin's personality, allowing him to engage in orgies of sex and alcohol. As a follower of the sect, Rasputin soon became known as a *staretz*, a man who attempted to rise to sainthood through sins of the flesh.

Rasputin first entered Russian history when he appeared mysteriously in St. Petersburg in 1903.

Charismatic, and speaking with the spiritual authority of a man on a divinely inspired mission, he made a deep impression on everyone he met. The aristocrats of St. Petersburg at that time were entertaining themselves by delving into spiritualism and the occult, so the mystic Rasputin was welcomed warmly.

From there it was not long before his fame reached the ears of the Tsar Nicholas II, later known as "Bloody Nicholas," a monarch with little experience and even less natural ability. Although kind and charming, Nicholas was not the right man to lead a crumbling empire with its rotting core, economic backwardness, restive population and centuries of tyranny. What was needed was a man of decisiveness, statesmanship, strength and vision. Personal concerns exacerbated Nicholas' problems, dividing his attention when it needed to be solely focused on saving his nation.

Years before his ascension to the throne, Nicholas had married his German cousin, Princess Alexandra of Hesse. Tsarina Alexandra's desire to produce an heir to the Russian throne was fulfilled in 1904 with the birth of Tsarevich Alexei. The joy of her triumph was dampened, however, when it was revealed that the baby was unwell: Alexei was hemophilic, prone to bouts of crippling illness and at the risk of bleeding to death from something as innocent as a paper cut. The tsarina was ridden with guilt over her son's potentially fatal affliction, and she grew to despise the court physicians who proved powerless to heal her beloved son. Emotionally torn and desperate for a means of curing Alexei, she turned to religion. What she needed was a miracle.

Just as the tsarina was at her lowest, Rasputin was ingratiating himself into Russia's aristocratic circles. With all other avenues explored and nowhere else to turn, in 1905 Nicholas and Alexandra summoned Rasputin to the imperial palace. Although they may have been dubious of this unwashed, wild-eyed man at first, they were won over when the mystic not only managed to staunch Alexei's bleeding but also somehow restored his vigour. The royal family was thrilled with the boy's recovery and became indebted to Rasputin. However, Rasputin direly warned them that the destiny of both the child and the royal dynasty were now irrevocably linked to him; if either was to survive, it would be because of his powers.

Now a fixture at court, Rasputin rapidly gained influence over the Romanovs and soon gained a say in government affairs. Rumours of his hold over Alexandra led the people of St. Petersburg to accuse the tsarina of sexual involvement with the Siberian monk. His mounting army of enemies claimed that Rasputin was nothing more than a self-seeking hypnotist exploiting the misfortunes of the royal family. While the hapless Nicholas fumbled with the reins of government, salacious rumours involving Rasputin quickly spread and blackened the name of both the tsar and tsarina.

In 1912, the royals urged Rasputin to visit the Holy Land in an effort to quell some of the controversy and appease those at court who resented the monk's influence in matters of government. With Rasputin gone, things did indeed settle down. The rumours quieted, and the Romanovs enjoyed a respite from the assault on their reputation. Unfortunately, the young tsarevich fell against the edge of his bathtub and began bleeding profusely. There was nothing any physician could do to stop the bleeding. In fear for her son's life, the frantic tsarina sent a telegram to Rasputin, begging him to do something to save Alexei. Rasputin wired back a simple message: "God has seen your tears. Do not grieve [for] the Little One will not die." A few hours after receiving the telegram, Alexei's bleeding stopped, and he began to immediately recover. The restoration of Alexei's health coincided with the restoration of Rasputin's position within the imperial court. Summoned from exile, he was once again part of the Romanovs' inner circle.

Rasputin reached the pinnacle of his political power after 1915, when Tsar Nicholas took personal command of his forces on the Eastern Front during World War I. The Russian army was having little success against the Germans, and Nicholas thought, wrongly as it turned out, that he could turn their fortunes around. Alexandra was left in charge of Russia's internal affairs, and Rasputin served as her personal adviser. His influence over her was such that many whispered the unkempt monk was actually in control of matters of state, a power behind the throne whispering in the ear of the weak tsarina.

Naturally, this outside influence outraged many aristocrats and politicians, but no one more than Grand Duke Dmitri Pavlovich and Prince Felix Yusupov, extended members of the Romanov royal family. In their view, the situation was intolerable and called for decisive action. Rasputin must die.

In December 1916, the conspirators invited Rasputin to the Yusupov palace for dinner. Rasputin was served a plate of pastries heavily laced with cyanide and then given a decanter of poisoned wine with which to wash it down. Incredibly, the poison didn't seem to faze him. When after two hours of gorging on cyanide-laced food and wine the monk complained of nothing more than a raw throat, the plotters knew they had to take more drastic measures.

Yusupov used his beautiful young wife Irina, the tsar's niece, as bait to lure the sexually insatiable monk into the palace's basement. Once there, the prince shot him through the heart. Rasputin staggered and jerked as a leaking red hole appeared in the centre of his chest. He collapsed, twitched for a few minutes, and then lay still. A physician among the conspirators felt for the monk's pulse and listened for a heartbeat. When he found neither, he declared Rasputin dead.

The conspirators left the body lying on the basement floor and went upstairs to celebrate their victory. A short while later Yusupov began to feel a little uneasy. Rasputin had demonstrated supernatural abilities before, and he had been incredibly difficult to kill tonight. What if the Mad Monk wasn't really dead? He went back down to the basement to make sure. To his horror, Yusupov watched as Rasputin's eyes twitched open and he slowly stumbled to his feet. Overwhelmed with terror, Yusupov was paralyzed, his feet rooted to the spot.

Eyes mad and rolling, lips peeled back to show stained and crooked teeth, Rasputin charged the prince. Shouting Yusupov's name in anger, he grabbed the prince by the shoulders and began to violently shake him. Yusupov was little more than a rag doll in Rasputin's iron grip, and he knew the man's superhuman strength could snap his neck with the barest of efforts.

Somehow, he managed to break free of Rasputin's hold and raced upstairs in search of help. Rasputin, meanwhile, had found his way out of the basement and was stumbling from the palace and threatening to tell about their treachery. The conspirators knew he had to be stopped, or their lives would be in danger from the vengeful tsarina. Gunshots rang out in the darkness. Rasputin was shot twice as he ran, once in the back and again in the head. Blood spurted forth, and Rasputin gurgled a bit as he wobbled, then sank down onto the cobblestones. Yet, incredibly, he was still alive, moaning pitifully. The conspirators beat Rasputin until they heard bone crack and saw his eyes roll back in their sockets.

Once again, the men checked the Mad Monk for any sign of life and, to their relief, found none. They were certain he was dead, but at the same time weren't taking any chances. After all, many people believed Rasputin to be the son of Satan himself. So they tightly bound his hands and feet, then wrapped the body in a heavy carpet and tossed it over a bridge railing into the waters of the Neva River. That, they were certain, was the end of the debased charlatan and his destructive influence on Russia.

Rasputin's frozen body was discovered the following day several kilometres downstream from where it had been dumped. The corpse was fished out of the water and pulled up on shore. Those retrieving the body were stunned at what they found. Rasputin had somehow shaken loose of the restraints binding his arms and legs, and had been trying to claw his way out of the icy water when he had finally died. Somehow, he had survived being totally submerged in freezing water for hours. It was determined that Rasputin's lungs were filled with water, proving that the mystic did not die of poisoning or of the multiple gunshot wounds or of the severe beating, but rather of drowning and perhaps hypothermia.

Numerous eyewitness reports then suggest the recovered body was set on fire. And this is where things get really weird. Accounts from the time say that Rasputin's body appeared to sit up in the flames as his body was consumed. His apparent attempts to escape the blaze thoroughly horrified bystanders.

Rasputin's claim to paranormal fame wasn't merely his unexplainable ability to heal the hemophilic tsarevitch when medicine could not and a seeming inability to be killed. He was also said to have supernatural strength beyond the ability of normal men. For example, he was said to have once killed two attackers by lifting them off the ground simultaneously and smashing their heads together. He then cast aside their lifeless bodies like they were little more than rag dolls. It was also claimed that he could make flowers bloom by holding them in his hand and make crippled men walk again through the power of his prayers. Even the most cynical of contemporary observers agreed Rasputin seemed to exercise genuine powers of prophecy and healing on several occasions.

His most astonishing prophecy came in the form of a letter to the tsarina written shortly before his assassination. In it, Rasputin hinted at real spiritual foresight. It read, in part: "I feel that I shall leave life before January 1st. If I am killed by common assassins…you [and the] Tsar of Russia have nothing to fear. [You will] remain on your throne and govern, and…your children will reign for hundreds of years in Russia…but if it is your relations who have wrought my death, then…none of your children or relations will remain alive for more than two years. They will be killed by the Russian people…" The letter was signed December 7, 1916. Twenty-three days later, Grigory Rasputin was dead, killed by two members of the Romanov family.

Not quite one year later, the October Revolution had toppled the monarchy. As the new Bolshevik government began the process of extricating Russia from the unpopular war, Nicholas II and his family were taken to Siberia and placed under guard. They remained there in exile until the middle of a chilly July night, when they were taken to the basement ostensibly to have their photograph taken. In a blaze of gunfire, the tsar, tsarina and their children were slaughtered. Just 19 months after Rasputin's death, his prophecy was fulfilled.

While some people would argue that Rasputin was little more than a charlatan with unusual charisma, others point to the circumstances of his death and the other unexplainable occurrences in his life as proof that he possessed supernatural abilities. If indeed he did enjoy unearthly abilities, what was their source?

The most common theory is that Rasputin was a mystic of some kind, a man who through dark faith or magic genuinely did possess the abilities for which history gives him credit. In this train of thought, the Mad Monk was no holy man, but rather a silk-tongued cultist who gained healing powers, precognition and the ability to mesmerize women directly from the devil. Certainly, there was no shortage of men in power who considered Rasputin to be the antichrist.

Others, however, have put forward the notion that he was the immortal known to medieval Europe as the Count de St. Germain, a mysterious figure who history can't decide to be fact or fiction. This theory suggests that Rasputin/St. Germain was working behind the scenes to manipulate events so that the Russian monarchy fell and revolution changed the nature of the Russian empire. When he found himself thrown into the icy surface of the river, Rasputin/St. Germain faced a dilemma. Although he could survive indefinitely without air and in the harshest of temperatures, to suddenly emerge alive and unscathed would have drawn unwanted attention. He decided that his best course of action was to fake his death. He endured the agony of a funeral pyre and the terror of being buried alive, later digging himself out of his grave to disappear once more into the mists of history.

Perhaps a bit out-there is the theory that Rasputin's supernatural abilities derived from the fact that he was not native to our world. Some UFOlogists believe that the Mad Monk was actually an alien from some distant planet. The theory goes that in the late 19th century, a small exploratory team of extraterrestrials came to Earth to study humanity. One member of this team went rogue and decided to indulge himself in a few years of carnal pleasure and political manipulation. Because his physiology was radically different—and presumably far more resilient—than ours, it proved very difficult for the conspirators to kill him. In addition, his possession of alien technology allowed him to perform what many people would consider miracles, including the healing of the young Romanov heir.

Finally, there is the idea that Rasputin was already dead when he was poisoned, shot, beaten and dumped in the river. Rasputin, you see, was a vampire. That would explain his power of suggestion over women, his ability to treat the hemophilic tsarevitch (presumably through feeding), and his unnatural resistance to injury and pain. It would also explain reports that Rasputin has been seen alive and well in the years since his "death."

But even if we accept that Rasputin was indeed mortal and was brutally killed one winter day in late 1916, it doesn't necessarily follow that he lies peacefully in his grave—does it? Indeed, there are many accounts to suggest that his unholy spirit has been spit up by the earth and continues to wreak havoc. The Mad Monk is as full of malice as ever, hateful and raging vengeance on those who claimed his life. Over the years, many people have encountered the murdered man's apparition, a spirit so evil that its very existence threatened their lives. Television star Alan Thicke shared his own terrifying encounter with Rasputin's dark spirit in a season four episode of *Celebrity Ghost Stories*. The experience, shared with his son, recording artist Robin Thicke, while visiting Russia, left the actor genuinely frightened and is enough to make one question the wisdom of a vacation to Rasputin's homeland.

Rasputin was an evil figure in life and is even viler in death. Even the bravest and most jaded ghost hunter should think twice about attempting to contact his spirit.

Three American teenagers lacked the good sense to leave the dead mystic alone. Their story is truly chilling.

In 2002, 16-year-old Jamie and her brother Jesse, one year her junior, moved with their family into a century-old home. The house had a cramped basement with an ancient furnace that rattled ominously, dingy corners full of shadows and spider webs, and a pervasive musty smell that didn't lift even when the tiny, grime-covered windows were slid open. The basement was, in a word, creepy. And the siblings loved it.

The strangest thing in the basement was a lone wooden door secured by an old padlock through a rusty latch. They often wondered what was behind that door, but it never went beyond contemplation to action. Their imaginations running wild, they dreamt up all kinds of chilling reasons why that door might be locked. It seemed better to leave well enough alone.

Then one day, Jesse's friend, Morgan, was over at the house. The three teenagers found themselves in the basement and contemplating what had become known as "The Door." Jesse and Morgan decided it was about time they saw what hid behind it.

"Wait," Jamie said as the two boys made for the doorway. "I have a bad feeling about this. Maybe we shouldn't open it. Maybe it's locked for a good reason."

But it was too late. They were already tugging on the padlock. After a few pulls, the rusty latch gave and pulled away from the wood. Jesse frowned at Jamie. "We might as well see what's inside," he said.

He turned the door handle. The heavy old door creaked as he pushed it open and flicked the closet light on.

All three teenagers squeezed into the doorway to see inside. And gasped in shock. The small, closet-sized room was empty except for a Ouija board lying on the dust-covered floor.

In the weeks that followed, the three kids dabbled with the board, but always during the day with the lights on, and always keeping the sessions short. Their confidence began to grow as they learned how to operate the Ouija and enjoyed moderate success.

Growing bold, Jesse and Morgan decided to contact spirits late one stormy night, with the lights out and the session illuminated only by the flickering light of a single candle. Jamie was nervous, and truthfully wanted no part of it, but was cajoled into participating. It was, Jamie admits today, the biggest mistake she has ever made.

The session began innocently enough, with the teenagers asking harmless questions of anonymous spirits and getting little in the way of response. A few simple yes or no questions were answered, but Jamie admits she wondered whether one of the boys was secretly manipulating the Ouija board.

It wasn't long before Morgan was growing bored and pushing for something a bit more exciting. "Why not contact the spirit of someone famous?" he asked, a mischievous smirk spreading across his face.

"Okay," Jesse responded. "Like who?"

"Rasputin."

Jesse and Jamie looked at one another. They knew a bit about the Russian mystic and his sinister reputation, but not enough to really cause them any pause at Morgan's suggestion. Shrugging their shoulders, they agreed.

That's when the evening turned terrifying. Morgan intoned the spirit of the dead monk, asking Rasputin to hear their summons and join them. There was a slight fluttering of the candle. When Morgan asked whether the Mad Monk was with them, the Ouija flew across the room and crashed against a wall. The candle began to dance wildly, and a strange shadow passed through the room.

A sudden feeling of terror ran through Jamie. She could feel fearful madness boring its way into her, leaving her flesh cold and goose-pimpled. Something seemed to reach down into her chest, slowly squeezing the air from her lungs, and she found herself gasping for breath. A vision passed sharply before her of a black-bearded man with penetrating eyes that flashed red with anger, a man so evil that his very existence threatened her life. For an instant she thought she would scream, but then all went black.

When Jamie came to she was lying on her back, her body limp as she broke out in a cold sweat. Jesse had seated himself quietly next to her, and a small smile crossed his face. He laid one hand on hers and patted it as one would a child. "You're all right," he said in a hushed whisper, though concern was evident on his face.

As Jamie regained her senses, she asked what had happened. The boys had watched helplessly as she fainted and the shadow hovered menacingly over her body. Neither one could move. Fear had rooted them to their spot. Dark claws had reached out to Jamie, and then she seemed to be enveloped in shadow as well.

Then, as quickly as it had appeared, the shadow had gone and the eerily silent, musty basement was all that remained. It had taken several minutes for Jamie's eyes to flutter open.

Although Morgan and Jesse later tried to dismiss the whole event as a product of their over-active imaginations, or at least told themselves that's all it was so they didn't have to deal with the terrifying truth, Jamie didn't have that luxury. She knew better. She knew the event had happened, and she had evidence to prove it. Painful bruises shaped like fingers had developed on her arms, inner thighs and breasts. Something had assaulted her that night, and she remains sure it was the spirit of the famously debauched Rasputin.

History tells us that the world was rid of Rasputin's evil almost a century ago. But don't be so sure. Numerous accounts suggest he is still terrorizing people to this day, and that his wraith is as full of malice as ever, seeking vengeance on those who claimed his life. In life, Rasputin was one of the scariest people ever to have existed. In death, his spirit is simply horrifying.

In Rasputin's case more than any other, it's best to let resting spirits lie.

An Uncle's Presence

"Katia," whose real name has been changed in print upon request, is no stranger to the supernatural. A young woman from England, she has a special gift. "All my life I've been able to see stuff the rest of my family can't see. No one else in my family really believes in this sort of stuff, only me," she says, somewhat self-consciously. But despite already having had several paranormal experiences, nothing could have prepared her for what awaited during a school trip to the French battlefields of World War I.

After the school group crossed the English Channel by ferry, they took a bus through northwestern France and settled into a youth hostel near the Belgian border. It was late and everyone was tired from the journey, so the students went almost immediately to their respective rooms, several of them to a room. Katia felt eerily chilled in the bedroom, shivering as the cold seeped deep into her body. As she reached for a sweater from her bag and snuggled under the blankets, Katia's friends all said they were warm and comfortable. Soon, lights were switched off, and one by one the girls nodded off to sleep.

"I woke up in the night at about three o'clock in the morning," recalls Katia. "I could hear the sound of a battle all around me. I remember hearing gun shots and explosions and cannon-like booms. At first I thought that the TV was on, but there was no way it could be that loud. I was really scared and could pick out screams and crying amid the artillery fire. Then they just stopped suddenly."

The next day, the school group travelled to Ypres, site of three of the most famous British battles in the First World War. For Katia, visiting the battlefield was a poignant and moving experience because she had a great-uncle who served with the Kings Royal Rifle Corps during the war and died during Passchendaele, the Third Battle of Ypres, fought from July 31 to November 6, 1917. Katia's uncle is interred in Ypres Reservoir Cemetery, and she was anxious to find his gravesite and pay her respects.

When at last Katia found the sombre white cross marking the grave, she was suddenly and inexplicably overcome by emotion for a man she never knew. With weak and shaky legs, she knelt by the stone and was surprised to find herself sobbing uncontrollably. She had a poppy to leave at the grave, but now she couldn't help but feel it was an insignificant gesture. After all her uncle had done for his country, and in light of his ultimate sacrifice, Katia felt a single poppy was a meagre offering.

"Then," Katia remembers, "I felt a warming presence around me that comforted me. It calmed me down and stopped me from crying. It made me feel contented and warm. The only way I can describe it is that it felt familiar." It was almost as if an unseen individual was laying a comforting arm around her shoulders. Katia instinctively knew the presence was the spirit of her dead great-uncle.

By the time Katia returned to the bus with her classmates, her sad mood had lifted, and she was in good spirits. As soon as everyone had climbed aboard, the bus ground into gear and moved on to other First World War battlefields where British soldiers fought and died. But even as Ypres receded in the bus's rearview mirror, Katia still felt the invisible presence at her side. The warming sensation never left her, almost protectively shielding her from the emotional weight of visiting more horrific battlefields. And she welcomed it; Katia had always been sensitive to the dead, and she questioned whether she would be strong enough when confronted by thousands of tormented, lonely, restless spirit-soldiers jostling for her attention all at once. In light of what transpired, it's possible the spirit was protecting her from something even worse.

For the rest of the day, Katia felt oddly detached from her friends. One of her classmates commented on how distracted she looked, and another questioned why she kept nervously looking behind her. How could she explain to them what she was experiencing? She couldn't, so she casually brushed off her friends' concerns. That night, when she crawled into bed, the warmth of her spirit companion remained with her. The chill she had felt the night before was kept at bay, and the cacophony of battlefield sounds—guns, explosions, the screams of the wounded and dying—was muted. Once, in the middle of the night, she awoke from her sleep to roll over. In that instant, she caught a fleeting glimpse of a shadow figure standing at the foot of her bed, a man composed entirely of darkness. Instead of being frightened, Katia felt safe and immediately fell back into a deep slumber. Her guardian stood watch over her throughout the night, granting her a restful reprieve from the echoes of war that threatened to overwhelm her senses. But Katia soon found out that he couldn't protect her from all of the horrors those battle-fields birthed.

The next day, the school group visited the trenches of the Somme, scene of one of the largest and most famous battles in World War I. On July 1, 1916, 10 British divisions attacked German lines along the River Somme. That first day of the offensive was the worst day in British military history, with 58,000 casualties. But despite the carnage, the attack continued, day after day, for weeks on end, to relieve the pressure on the French troops fighting desperately in the Battle of Verdun. When at last the British offensive was called off on November 18 and the Battle of the Somme drew to a close, more than 1 million men had been killed or wounded, making it one of humanity's bloodiest battles.

Katia felt uncomfortable as soon as she stepped off the bus. It had been raining for the past couple of days, and the trenches were muddy and wet—just as they would have been nearly a century ago during the battle itself. A chilly mist hovered over the battlefield, creating an unearthly hush.

Katia took lots of pictures of her friends in the trenches where soldiers would have waited nervously to go "over the top" to attack the Germans. All of her pictures later came out flawless—all except those taken in the Canadian trenches. In those photos, strange glowing orbs appeared around her friends. Some were stationary; others left streaks of light in their wake as they whizzed past. None of the students had seen anything out of the ordinary. The orbs look nothing like droplets of rain, though the reader may dismiss them as such. There is no rational explanation, however, for what followed.

As the group began to filter away, moving on to the next location on the battlefield, Katia and a male friend remained behind to take a few more pictures. She posed her friend, took a dozen paces back, aimed her camera—and let out a shrill scream of terror. Standing behind her friend was the misty image of a soldier.

Alerted by her scream and wide-eyed stare, Katia's friend turned to look behind him. He recoiled in fright. The apparition came closer, his features growing clearer and monstrous. Both students were horrified at the sight of a bloody stump of mangled flesh and bone where his right arm had been blown away…the skeletal face with deep, empty eye sockets…the fat, brown worms curling from an open, toothless mouth.

And then they ran. Katia's shoes thudded hard on the ground. Her lungs felt like they would burst, but she kept running. She heard her friend running right behind her. Back at the bus, with the apparition far behind them, she finally started to breathe again, sucking in long, cold breaths.

"I didn't sleep at all that night at the hostel," Katia says, remembering how the cold chill of terror only slowly lifted from her body. "I still felt the presence, but it felt a bit more distant that night. When I got on the ferry the next day to cross back to England, the presence seemed to disappear, and I have never felt the same presence at home. But I am still petrified whenever I think of the [other] man."

The experience was several years ago, but the memory remains fresh. It still terrifies her when she thinks about it late at night, when darkness settles over the world and wind rattles the window panes. Her visit to the battlefields of France brought her face to face with a horror the likes of which she had never before imagined possible. But, despite the nightmares and cold sweats that continue to plague her, Katia doesn't regret her decision to visit France. It was during that school trip that she connected—in a very real sense—with the spirit of a great-uncle she had never known. She would always treasure that opportunity.

Shadows of Singapore

The wind sighed. The woman, aware of the stories surrounding the jungle temple, furtively looked around. There was nothing to worry about, she told herself, trying to calm her nerves. A paranormal investigator, she had driven up from Singapore in an attempt to connect with the spirit believed to be bound to this holy site, and she wasn't going to let rumours of hungry shadows and demonic possession frighten her away.

She began walking up the hill, her mind going over the methods she would use in her spirit communication. She was so focused on her thoughts that she nearly bumped right into a child. The little girl's long, blonde hair fell over her face, hiding it from view; she wore a thin dress and stood motionless in the middle of the path.

"Excuse me," the paranormal investigator gasped, startled by the girl's sudden appearance. "I didn't see you there."

And then a gust of wind blew the hair away from the girl's face. The investigator stared into the face of death: pale and clammy flesh, cavernous black eye sockets, no lips over broken teeth. The ghost girl took a silent step toward the investigator and reached out a bony hand…

The horrors surrounding this particular temple are well documented. It involves the tragic death of a young girl, her corpse feasted upon by vermin and deprived of a proper burial; a restless spirit unable to find solace beyond the grave; figures of darkness that prey upon the living; and evil cults seeking to worship and gain power from fiendish spirits. It's a story of both tragedy and terror.

In the years prior to the outbreak of World War I, a German merchant and his family settled on a coffee plantation on the island of Pulau Ubin (the name translates as "Rock Island") in the British colony of Malaya. Those were joyful and prosperous days. The merchant grew wealthy on his crops, watched as his family expanded with each successive birth of a new child, and was invigorated by the tropical warmth and the lushness of the beautiful jungle. Although he was proud of his nation of birth, this island was his home now, and he wanted nothing to do with anything that might upset his new way of life. If war came—and increasingly it looked like it would—he vowed to remain aloof from it. Europe was far away, after all, and what concern was it of his if the countries there decided to come to blows? Sadly, though the German merchant wanted nothing to do with the war, the war found him nonetheless.

In August 1914, at the outset of the war, British soldiers arrived at his home. They informed the merchant that his ownership of the land was voided and that they were confiscating the plantation in the name of the Crown. The merchant argued, the soldiers grew threatening, and the scene grew tense.

Watching the confrontation unfold was the German's young daughter, a girl of about six or seven. She was terrified by the fierce-looking men carrying guns and threatening her father, and she recognized fear and anger in her father's face and voice. She didn't understand much of what was being said, but she understood that her father was in some sort of trouble.

The girl did what so many children do when they are afraid: she ran. With tears streaking down her chubby cheeks, she raced deep into the jungle. She ran blindly, not knowing or caring what direction she was heading, just so long as she left those frightening soldiers behind. She only stopped when her chest ached, her legs quivered and her breath came in desperate gasps. She sat on the ground beneath a big tree, hugged her knees to her chest and cried.

After a while, the crying subsided and the shaking stopped. Only then, when she had time to look around at her surroundings, did she realize that she was lost and that darkness was quickly settling over the jungle. Now a different type of fear began to overwhelm her: fear of the monstrous beasts that lurked in the jungle at night. Rising to her feet, the girl began pushing through the foliage, heading in a direction she hoped would bring her home. Soon, the sun had sunk below the horizon and the blackness of the night shrouded the landscape. The poor young girl could not see her hand before her face, let alone what lay ahead as she plowed through the under-brush. She never saw the precipice. She just felt herself falling and had time only for a brief scream of terror before her life ended on the jagged rocks below.

What this little girl didn't know was that the planta-tion to which she had been trying to return was no lon-ger her home. The British soldiers had taken her family into custody and placed them under heavy guard. They were citizens of an enemy nation; therefore, their loyalty was under suspicion. They languished for the duration of the war in a prisoner-of-war camp, their ownership of the land considered forfeit. The soldiers made only a half-hearted attempt to search for the missing girl before concluding she had fallen prey to a predator and been swallowed up by the jungle.

The plantation's Malay workers, who had been treated well by the landowner and who had all been charmed by his youngest daughter, wouldn't give up the search so easily. They scoured the jungle, holding out hope that they might find the girl alive. It wasn't to be. After a few days of searching, her broken body was found at the base of the cliff. It was covered in a swarm of vicious termites, however, and no one could get close to her without feeling the fiery pain of countless tiny bites. The corpse couldn't be moved, so the workers simply threw soil over it as a form of burial. After that, whenever any of them passed that spot, they would be sure to say a prayer to ensure the girl's spirit remained at peace despite her improvised burial.

She wouldn't remain in the shallow grave forever. A couple of years later, her remains were exhumed and placed in a Chinese temple atop a hill on the island. Gamblers began to pray at the temple for good luck. Several of them were so successful they were certain their good fortune was the result of being blessed by the spirit of the dead German girl.

When the war was over, British officials freed the German merchant and his family. Although he would never recover his plantation, before leaving for Germany, he did return to Pulau Ubin to find out what had happened to his daughter. He left disappointed. Whether because of language difficulties or because the locals were unwilling to part with what was by now considered a relic of good fortune, the grieving father was never told where his daughter's body rested. He left Singapore without answers and without a body to bury in his native Germany.

The skeletal remains of the young girl were enshrined at the temple until 1974, when the property became the site of a granite quarry. To make room for the quarry, the old temple was to be demolished and a new one built. The girl's remains, by then little more than some bone fragments and a few locks of hair, along with an iron cross and some coins, were reverently placed in a porcelain urn and buried in the soil. An altar was built over the resting site, and the new temple was erected around this focal point.

Here's where things take a turn for the mysterious. Many people believe the porcelain urn is in fact empty. It's been suggested that the young girl's remains were stolen by occultists. These modern-day witches believed the hair and bone fragments were extremely strong with spiritual energy, which they wanted to harness for their own dark magic. Who knows where this poor girl's remains are today, what evil they have helped perpetrate and what unholy abuses they have endured.

Even though the physical remains of the girl are likely no longer in the temple, worshippers believe part of her soul remains tied to that building and continue to flock there to pray to her. They leave offerings of perfume, cosmetics, mirrors, flowers and fruit in her name. They ardently believe she can give blessings to those of them with pure hearts who are in dire need of good fortune.

The young girl's spirit is considered an almost angelic figure, yet frightening and inexplicable things have been reported in and around the temple. Is she targeting people with darkness in their souls, people who seek to exploit or misuse her generosity, or has she been twisted, tainted or angered by the occult rituals that her physical remains have undergone?

The Singapore Paranormal Investigators, for example, have received numerous reports that people have encountered moving shadows outside the temple at night. These shadows should not have been there. Human-shaped, though distorted, they had no natural source. It was as if they had detached themselves from their living hosts to wander freely. They are reported to slink about in the darkness, retreating hastily when the beam of a flashlight strikes them, almost as if the light terrifies or wounds them in some fashion.

How these undead silhouettes are connected to the deceased girl is a matter of speculation. Perhaps they are the souls of worshippers determined to guard the sacred shrine. Maybe they are the girl's family, trying vainly to connect with her in the afterlife. Or might it be possible they were somehow conjured by the dark rituals performed on her bones?

The idea of dark reflections of the deceased lurking about in the shadows of the pale moonlight is frightening enough, but more sinister happenings have been reported at the shrine. Some people say the shadows stretch out from the dark with impossibly long arms ending in misshapen claws that, when they rake across a person's flesh, not only leave angry red scratches but also sap the individual of vitality. For days afterward, the victim is lethargic, weak, sleepy and sometimes even bedridden with feebleness.

Recently, members of a film crew who reenacted the legend of the ill-fated German girl for a movie production were said to become possessed. One vomited repeatedly after touching the urn, and the other, who was dressed as the little girl, suddenly started to speak in German even though she had no knowledge of that language. Understandably, the entire film crew was deeply disturbed by the incident.

Good fortune greets most who worship at the temple on Pulau Ubin, but not everyone is so lucky. For some, a visit to this sacred location is the stuff of nightmares. Malicious shadow apparitions, debilitating illness, unwelcome possession by restless spirits and terrifying encounters with wraiths that have crawled up from the grave combine to horrify the unlucky...or the unworthy. No one knows exactly why some who come to the temple are favoured and others are greeted only by terror. It's just one of many mysteries associated with the temple.

One thing is certain: the death of the plantation owner's daughter was a tragedy. An even greater tragedy is the disrespect and abuse to which her remains have been subjected. Is it surprising that her soul finds it impossible to rest easy?

The Forlorn Cabin

The woods that early spring day had an almost mystical feel; the bare branches of the trees swayed back and forth in the breeze. To the woman walking amidst them, it appeared almost as though the trees were speaking in sign language, giving a silent warning of what lay ahead for her. Something wasn't right, but she couldn't put a finger on what was wrong.

The atmosphere suddenly felt heavy and unnatural. The air grew frigid, even though the sun was still shining in a clear blue sky. As the chill grew more intense, the woman found it almost impossible to keep warm. She pulled her hat lower over her ears and buried her gloved hands in her pockets, but the cold seemed to bite right through the wool and penetrate straight to her bones. Her eyes began searching the woods, looking for the presence she sensed lurking behind the trees.

Throwing a quick glance at her partner, the woman noted that he didn't seem bothered in the least by the cold, the eerie atmosphere that had suddenly settled over the woodland or the presence of the trailing spirit.

Then she froze as still as a statue. Looming in the trees nearby, as grey as a tombstone, was the ethereal figure of a young man long dead who resented the intrusion on his privacy. He was well-groomed and well-dressed, and he might have been pleasant-looking if not for those deep, dark holes where his eyes should have been. Maybe she shouldn't have come down this forgotten road after all…

About an hour's drive north of Toronto, Ontario, is an overgrown laneway that runs deep into regenerated woods.

The original road to the town of Orangeville, it begins opposite a weathered one-time general store in the heart of the ghost town of Ballycroy—a forgotten highway running through a forgotten community. Hidden by the weeds and trees on either side of the road is a series of foundation holes, all that remains of the homes and businesses that once stood there.

We visited in 2002, almost a century after Ballycroy's abandonment, in preparation for an article detailing the history of the vanished village, never anticipating the intimate connection we would make with the past. It was early spring, and despite the crystal blue sky and bright sun above, patches of snow stubbornly lingered here and there in the shade. Leaving the car behind, we began to walk into the bush along the old road to Orangeville. We could see curbing from the original road through the tall brown grass. The ground was still hard with frost, making it difficult to walk. That day, it felt like the distance we travelled was measured in years instead of kilometres.

After we had walked perhaps a kilometre or two, we stopped. Neither of us could believe our eyes when the shadowy form of a lone cabin suddenly appeared between the dark pines and skeletal maples. There was something oddly unsettling about the cabin, almost as if it had purposefully hidden itself away from civilization and resented the intrusion of human eyes. It sagged with the weight of the ages; the wood was weathered grey and rotting, and the shingles were peeling from the roof. The windows had been boarded up with thick plywood. Under a moody grey sky or in the failing light of dusk, an overactive imagination might cause one to wonder whether the windows were boarded to keep intruders out or to imprison whatever unspeakable things that might have made their home within.

Feeling an irresistible urge to enter, we climbed through the lone un-boarded window and inhaled an overwhelming musty smell. The stink hung in the air with the unsettled dust our entrance had kicked up. No one had been there for a long time; that much was immediately obvious. With only a hint of sunlight filtering in, it was difficult to see, so we proceeded cautiously. We noted how small the rooms were and that several belongings—including steel frame beds, a lumpy mattress, an old kitchen stove and several rusted tin cans—remained littered about.

Maria started to become uneasy, and the musty air was causing her difficulty in breathing. What began as mild discomfort developed so that each rasping breath she took rattled painfully in her chest.

It's believed that the ghost of a soldier killed in France in 1917 returned home to this forlorn, forgotten cabin in Ontario.

"At first, I just tasted something foul in my throat. It was like something rotten. It tasted like death. Then I started to actually have a hard time catching my breath," Maria recalled later. "I hate spitting. I think it's a rude habit. But my discomfort was so intense that I felt I simply had to spit out whatever it was that was in my throat."

I didn't learn until much later that Maria's shortness of breath was caused by an oppressive feeling rather than stale air. Maria felt we had overstayed our welcome in the little cottage. She instinctively sensed that someone invisible to our eyes was upset that we had intruded upon his solace and wanted us gone, and she knew it was unwise to linger any longer than we already had. It was clearly time to go.

Does the spirit of a World War I soldier hover behind the sign announcing the town he once called home?

We climbed out through the window, jumped to the ground and retraced our steps back to the car. Maria was unusually silent throughout the walk. Little did I know that her silence was a result of struggling with the weight of the unnerving experience she had just endured in the cabin, and of the unsettling certainty that we were being watched by someone, something, following us unseen in the woods.

Before we got into the car, Maria decided to take a few last photographs by which to remember our day of exploration. She took a few of the false-fronted general store, and then she took one final photo of the faded sign announcing Ballycroy.

A few days later, the photos were developed, and I noticed something unusual: the image of the sign was unnaturally dark, much more so than those taken just minutes earlier. In fact, it was almost sepia-toned, as if it had been taken in the 19th century. The colourless starkness of the photo was in direct contrast to the bright, cloudless day we both remembered. Perplexed, I made an offhand comment to Maria, something to the effect of, "It's almost as though someone didn't want us to take this picture."

Maria almost immediately noticed the spectral figure of a man standing behind the sign, and once she pointed it out, I agreed the image was unmistakable. That's when Maria opened up and shared her experience within the derelict cottage. We wondered whether a spectral denizen of the cabin had followed us back to our car. The thought was admittedly a bit disturbing.

Other people we have shown the photo to have seen the shape without prompting, including many who were skeptical about the existence of ghosts. But who was this spectral figure? Who was it who resented our intrusion and chased us from the cabin? Who didn't want us to take that snapshot of the Ballycroy sign? It was time to investigate the history of that weary cottage.

Although oppressive today, the cabin's origins are decidedly normal. In the late 19th century, the cottage was the homestead of the Pettit family, headed by John and Margaret. They were simple farmers, unassuming and humble—the kind of folks one would like to think good things happen to. They worked the land, raised their children the best way they knew, attended church and asked for nothing other than what their farm and their Lord could provide. Surely good fortune should have been theirs. Fate doesn't always follow such logic. Records show that the Pettit family suffered a terrible tragedy in 1917, and it is possible that that tragedy still stains their home all these years later.

As it did for so many families, the First World War brought the Pettit family pain and loss. In 1916, Chester Pettit, who grew up in the tiny three-room cabin, enlisted in the Canadian army and was promptly shipped to France for front-line duty. He never returned home. Chester Pettit died in the mud, barbed wire and shell holes of Vimy Ridge in 1917. It's believed he perished choking from poison gas, writhing in agony as his lungs burned. Undoubtedly, his final thoughts were of home and the loved ones he would never again see.

Or did Chester in fact return home to his family, in spirit if not in body? Some, these authors included, have come away believing that his spirit haunts the abandoned and derelict Pettit cabin to this day.

Was the choking discomfort Maria experienced the psychic residue of Chester Pettit's final moments? Perhaps there was something more toxic than mould and dust in the cabin: the spirit of someone long dead but grown foul with restlessness.

Adding to the chilling nature of the entire experience was Maria's description of the entity she had sensed in the building: tall with broad shoulders, dark hair, aged early to mid-thirties. This description, we would learn months later after extensive research, matched the surviving photographs of Chester Pettit almost perfectly.

Had we inadvertently disturbed Pettit by trespassing in his domain? It was almost unbelievable: the uncanny coincidences, the strange happenings, the inexplicable feelings. We were shocked, excited and a little frightened at the same time. To write about ghosts is one thing; to experience them is something else altogether.

We aren't the only ones who have experienced the supernatural in and around the Pettit cottage. Many people who venture down the old road speak of a foreboding feeling that grows more intense the nearer they draw to the aged cabin. Ballycroy resident Dave Bond once witnessed a shadowy figure, a vaguely man-shaped apparition composed entirely of blackness, in the woods and confirms that the area is tainted by spectral energies that sometimes manifest as ghost lights. One eyewitness claims to have actually seen Chester Pettit standing before him, ethereal but otherwise distinct. The dead man's jaw creaked open and a mournful groan escaped, chasing the witness away.

Removed from the advance of civilization and surrounded by land with an almost timeless feel to it, Ballycroy is one of the best-preserved ghost towns in Central Ontario. Time seems to stand still there, and as long as it does, it seems likely that Chester Pettit will remain. What happens to the restless spirit if the land is eventually developed is anyone's guess.

The Tomb of the Unknown Soldier

Sunlight streaming through a window awoke the man from a restless sleep, and he reluctantly sat up, groaning as his head exploded in protest. Rubbing the sting from his eyes, he leaned forward on his bed to stretch a back aching from too many hours spent lying upon it. He was hungry, filthy, hungover and angry at himself for falling so far. It sickened him to think about what he had let himself become. He'd once been a British soldier, an officer, a member of one of the proudest regiments in the entire army. But all that changed during the Great War. He could still see the faces of the young men who he'd led to their deaths in France.

He shook away the memories that haunted him, then stood and slowly began to put on a uniform bedecked with medals and other reminders of a distinguished career. He looked at himself in the mirror and didn't recognize the man looking back. Once a tall, straight and confident soldier, he had been reduced to a mere shadow of his former self. He felt like a fraud wearing the uniform, like the jacket and its distinctions belonged to someone else. He felt ill, but he had promised—promised that he would put aside his self-loathing for a few hours to pay respect to his fallen comrades at the Tomb of the Unknown Soldier.

A few hours later found him standing outside Westminster Abbey, rooted to the spot by guilt at having survived the war when so many men, men he felt were better deserving than he, had died. Finally, though they were quivering almost uncontrollably, his legs began to carry him forward. He pushed through the doors and slowly made his way toward the monument, the echoing of his footsteps sounding impossibly loud in the cavernous building. The tomb came into sight.

The former soldier stopped. His eyes welled over, and tears streamed unhindered down his face. Before him, standing at full attention, dressed in their military finest, was every one of the young men who had been killed under his command. The man felt a surge of pride he hadn't felt in years. He drew himself up to his full height and snapped a crisp salute. Nodding, slight smiles upon faces that will forever remain young, the ghostly soldiers faded from view.

Although they had lost their lives, the undead soldiers had saved his, the man knew. That day was the last time he cried for his fallen comrades. From then on, it became his mission, his obligation, as he saw it, to live life to the fullest in their honour. Anything less would be a disservice to their sacrifice and their memory. Such is the spiritual power of Westminster Abbey's Tomb of the Unknown Soldier.

Westminster Abbey is best known for the elaborate coronations of English kings and queens, a tradition dating back centuries. This sacred structure, as beautiful as it is historic, is one of the most celebrated buildings in all of Britain. It has one more honorific: as befits a place of worship that houses the remains of deceased kings and queens and the greatest heroes of the realm, Westminster Abbey is London's most haunted church.

With such a long and storied history, it would be odd if the abbey were to be without any illustrious ghosts. It should come as little surprise that almost from the time it was built there have been reports of apparitions and other phenomena in its cavernous interior. Among Westminster Abbey's ghosts is a priest who holds conversations with churchgoers before silently vanishing into the walls, and a cowled monk who shuffles across the floor on tired legs, his face hidden in his hood. The most recent of Westminster Abbey's restless spirits is the figure of a First World War soldier who stands sentinel over one of the most poignant war memorials in all of Britain: the Tomb of the Unknown Soldier.

During World War I, over 116,000 British servicemen lost their lives on foreign battlefields, from the desolate trenches of France to the cold, grey waters of the Atlantic to the sands of the Middle East. One of the greatest tragedies of the war was that it proved impossible to recover all of the bodies for a proper burial on home soil, and identification of many of the remains was nearly impossible. Thousands of men were buried in mass graves with unmarked headstones or were never found at all. In the postwar period, the British government decided to build a symbolic grave and monument to the brave young men who gave up their lives for their country yet have no known grave.

On the night of November 7, 1920, six unidentified bodies were exhumed from four different battlefield graves on France's Western Front (Aisne, Somme, Arras and Ypres). Each corpse was solemnly wrapped in a Union Jack flag and then taken to a small military chapel at St. Pol, near Arras. There, a British representative, Brigadier General L.J. Wyatt, selected one set of remains at random to serve as the Unknown Soldier. The general had no idea of the ranks of the fallen soldiers or from which battlefield they had been exhumed. The corpse hidden beneath the Union Jack may have been a private or a general, a humble colonial farmer or the blue-blooded son of an English aristocrat. In this instance, all soldiers were equal. The selected body, known henceforth as the Unknown Soldier, was transported back to Britain, while the others were returned to the battlefields from which they came and were reburied in their respective graves.

The Unknown Soldier's body was sealed in an English-made coffin and arrived at Dover aboard HMS *Verdun* on November 10. Later that day, the coffin was taken by train to London. The following day, November 11, the Unknown Soldier arrived at Westminster Abbey, where the fallen warrior was honoured by King George V and given a royal funeral full of pomp and ceremony. The casket was laid to rest in soil brought from the French battlefields and under a marble slab quarried in Belgium. The text on the tomb reads, "They buried him among the kings, because he had done good toward God and toward his house."

In the months after the funeral, over one million people visited the tomb. Even today, it is one of the most visited graves in the world. But it seems not all of the visitors to the monument are among the living.

When the crowds thin and silence settles over the church, the ghostly apparition of a soldier appears next to the grave. The ghost's description varies among witnesses.

Some describe him as being muddy, wounded and weary. Other eyewitnesses state the spectral soldier is youthful, vigorous and wearing full dress uniform. In any event, he stands in silence, facing the monument, his head bowed in respect for the noble service of those who died in battle. Then, after a few moments of prayer, the spirit simply fades away.

On rare occasions, the apparition does more than stand silent sentinel. People have seen him walking slowly through the church with one hand outstretched, his eyes downcast, apparently in search of something he can never find. He causes no harm, but his passage chills the air with palpable sadness. Although the Tomb of the Unknown Soldier is located at the west end of the nave of Westminster Abbey, the ethereal soldier wanders freely throughout the interior of the church before fading from view or passing through a stone wall. Sometimes, the soldier isn't seen at all, but his footsteps are heard near the tomb, marching in perfect military precision.

Is this ghost that of the unidentified soldier who lies buried in Westminster Abbey, or is the apparition just one of the hundreds of thousands of soldiers who fought for King and Country during the First World War who simply materializes there to honour the dead? We'll never know.

Eyewitnesses aren't shy about their encounters with the spectral soldier at Westminster Abbey. People have been seeing him for almost a century, after all—and Westminster's other spirits for hundreds of years before that—so there can be no fear of ridicule.

A few years back, a group of tourists approaching the tomb were impressed to find half a dozen soldiers standing in a straight row before it. Dressed in khaki uniforms with rifles held against their shoulders, they appeared to be standing solemn guard with eyes staring unflinchingly ahead. The soldiers remained completely inert, but otherwise appeared as flesh and blood as you or I. The only thing betraying their otherworldly nature was their unmoving gazes, which produced a slightly unnerving sense of watchfulness. The visitors took out their cameras and snapped a few shots of the soldiers. Imagine their surprise when they returned home and developed the pictures to find not a soul appeared in any of the images—the pictures were crisp and clean, the Tomb of the Unknown Soldier was clearly visible, but the squad of attentive soldiers was conspicuously absent.

There are countless paranormal tales associated with the Tomb of the Unknown Soldier, but every so often, a story emerges that is so touching as to stand out from the rest. One such story was provided by a Thea, a resident of the English town of Lewes:

> *My grandmother and grandfather married at a very young age and had four children before my grandfather was 24 years old. They didn't have much, but they did have each other. Then my grandfather enlisted to fight in the war, leaving my grandmother and their children behind. My grandmother missed him terribly. She loved lilacs because they were the first flowers my grandfather had ever given her, and so she would wear perfume that smelled of lilac to remind her of him while he was fighting. Unfortunately, he never returned home.*

He died somewhere in France. My grandmother was devastated. She never really got over the loss, and she continued to wear that perfume for the rest of her life. The smell of lilacs would linger for minutes after she had left a room.

Years after my grandmother had passed away, my mother visited the Tomb of the Unknown Soldier while in London one day. She saw a soldier standing near the tomb. She went pale as the colour drained from her face, and her heart pounded fiercely in her chest. The soldier looked eerily familiar; he resembled the sepia-toned picture of her father that had always hung in its oval frame in the family living room. My mother had been too young to have memories of her father, which left a void that could never be filled. She stared at this soldier, who seemed motionless and almost statue-like. He looked just like her father, or at least as he appeared in that old photograph. She was still staring when the soldier faded away before her very eyes. But before he disappeared, my mom swore that for a second they locked eyes, and he smiled slightly.

The experience troubled my mom for days. Had she seen her long-dead father, a father she had never known and couldn't picture without a photograph? One night, she sat in her chair by the fire and asked her mother for a sign. Had that been Dad? The distinctive scent of lilac suddenly whiffed into the room. This was in the middle of winter, so there were no lilacs or any other flowers. The smell lingered, leaving no doubt in my mom's mind. It was a message from my grandmother. My mom had finally met her father, more than 40 years after he died. It was one of her fondest memories, and every time she told it, her eyes welled with tears.

The Tomb of the Unknown Soldier moves many people to the verge of tears. Even those who have no connection to the war cannot help but feel the weight of the sacrifice and loss that hangs solemnly over the monument. One hundred years have passed since World War I began, but the pain and loss of that terrible conflict is not so easily gotten over.

The Tomb of the Unknown Soldier is one of the most poignant and emotional locations in all of Britain. Unveiled to commemorate those who perished in the First World War, it has come to symbolize the loss and sheer tragedy of that conflict. There is a distinct heaviness in the air around the memorial that is palpable, moving and sometimes unsettling. Making the memorial all the more heart-wrenching is the appearance of the ghostly soldier who has been unable to find the peace he justly deserves. Is he chained to our mortal plane by the untimely nature of his death, or is he fulfilling a greater purpose? Perhaps he is duty bound to stand vigil over the Tomb of the Unknown Soldier so as to remind us to honour the dead of the Great War. If so, it's a noble legacy.

Sources

Asfar, Dan. *Haunted Battlefields*. Edmonton, AB: Lone Pine Publishing, 2004.

Belanger, Jeff. *Encyclopedia of Haunted Places: Ghostly Locales from Around the World*. Franklin Lakes, NJ: New Page Books, 2005.

Bird, Will. *Ghosts Have Warm Hands*. Toronto: Clark, Irwin, 1968.

Brooks, J.A. *Britain's Haunted Heritage*. Norwich, UK: Jarrold Publishing, 1990.

Carrington, Hereward. *Psychical Phenomena and the War*. New York: Exposition Press, 1975.

Clarke, David. *The Angel of Mons: Phantom Stories and Ghostly Guardians*. West Sussex, UK: Wiley, 2004.

Colombo, John Robert. *Mysteries of Ontario*. Toronto: Hounslow Press, 1999.

Cook, Tim. "Grave Beliefs: Stories of the Supernatural and the Uncanny among Canada's Great War Trench Soldiers." *The Journal of Military History*. Vol. 77, No. 2. Lexington, VA: Society of Military History, 2013.

Da Silva, Maria and Andrew Hind. *Ghosts of Niagara-on-the-Lake*. Toronto: Dundurn, 2009.

Da Silva, Maria and Andrew Hind. *More Ontario Ghost Stories*. Edmonton, AB: Ghost House Books, 2013.

Everett, Susanne, Peter Young and Robin Sommer. *Wars of the 20th Century*. London: Bison Books, 1985.

Farnthorpe, Lionel and Patricia. *The World's Most Mysterious People*. Toronto: Hounslow Press, 1998.

Gribble, Leonard. *Famous Historical Mysteries*. London: Target Books, 1974.

Hauck, Dennis William. *The International Directory of Haunted Places*. London: Penguin Books, 2000.

Jarvis, Dale. *Haunted Shores: True Ghost Stories of Newfoundland and Labrador*. St. John's, NL: Flanker Press, 2004.

Jones, Richard. *Haunted Britain and Ireland*. London: New Holland Publishers, 2001.

Jones, Richard. *Haunted Houses of Britain and Ireland*. London: New Holland Publishers, 2005.

Mechem, Liz. *Disasters at Sea: A Visual History of Infamous Shipwrecks*. Long Island City, NY: Hammond World Atlas Corporation, 2009.

Nicolle, David. *Crécy 1346: Triumph of the Longbow*. London: Osprey Publishing, 2000.

O'Sullivan, Patrick. *The Lusitania: Unraveling the Mysteries*. London: Collins Press, 1998.

Ronayne, Ian. *Jersey War Walks*. Bradford-on-Avon, UK: Seaflower Books, 2012.

Roper, Michael. *The Secret Battle: Emotional Survival in the Great War*. Manchester, UK: Manchester University Press, 2009.

Rutkowski, Chris and Geoff Dittman. *The Canadian UFO Report*. Toronto, ON: Dundurn Group, 2006.

Schmalenbach, Paul. *German Raiders: A History of Auxiliary Cruisers of the German Navy 1895–1945.* Annapolis, MD: Naval Heritage Press, 1979.

Smith, Barbara. *Ghosts Stories of the Sea.* Edmonton, AB: Lone Pine Publishing, 2003.

The Times History of the War. Volume XI. London: London Times, 1916

Upton, Kyle. *Haunted Niagara II.* Niagara-on-the-Lake, ON: Self-published, 2004.

Wood, Alan C. *Military Ghosts.* Stroud, UK: Amberley Publishing, 2009.

Acknowledgements

We would like to thank everyone who helped us make this book a reality, the most important of whom are the individuals who came forward to share their own brushes with the supernatural. Without them, this book would not have been possible, and the fascinating, haunted heritage associated with the First World War would remain hidden in the past. As we celebrate the centenary of the war, these stories of ghosts and the paranormal are particularly relevant and deserve to be remembered. So to all those who provided first-hand experiences, thank you.

Many others proved helpful during the research process. Most notable were the museums, libraries and historical associations that lent pictures and the resources that ensured the history behind these stories was portrayed as accurately as possible.

Lastly, we want to thank all the men—and, so often forgotten today, women as well—who served their countries during this horrific war. Far too many made the ultimate sacrifice, and even those who returned were not unscarred, the physical and mental wounds being slow to heal. This book honours their service. Their tragic and haunting tales teach us to enjoy and appreciate life help us to believe that there may be existence beyond death.

Personal Acknowledgement

Andrew writes: I want to thank my grandfather, Arthur Hind, for kick-starting my interest in military history, which I trace back to countless hours spent watching John Wayne World War II movies at his side. I hope he's proud of "little Andy." I also want to express my undying gratitude to Maria for her friendship and all that she brings to my craft and to my life.

About the Authors

Maria Da Silva and **Andrew Hind** are freelance writers who specialize in the paranormal, history and travel. They have a passion for bringing to light unusual stories, chilling tales of the supernatural, little-known historical episodes and fascinating locations few people know about. Together, they have contributed numerous articles to magazine publications and newspapers, including the *Toronto Star, Lakeland Boating, Horizons, Canada's History, Muskoka Magazine* and *Paranormal Magazine*. This is their fourth book in the Ghost House Books series; their preceding titles were *Cottage Country Ghosts, Even More Ontario Ghost Stories* and *Ghost Stories of the War of 1812. Ghost Stories of the First World War* represents Maria and Andrew's sixteenth book together.

Maria has always been captivated by ghosts and the paranormal, and she regularly explores the subject through her writing. Andrew developed a love of history early on, and he hopes, through his books with Maria, to develop a similar passion in others. He has a special interest in military history.

Maria and Andrew speak frequently at public forums about their work and passions. They also conduct guided historical and ghost tours that help people connect with the past in a personal way, most notably at Bracebridge, Ontario's Inn at the Falls and Muskoka Heritage Place in Huntsville, Ontario.

Maria and Andrew reside in Bradford, Ontario.